PASTIES, SAFFRON BUNS AND MURDER

With Recipes

The Cornish Village
Mysteries Book 1

Clara Penrose

ISBN-13: 9798389049505
ISBN-10: 9798389049505

Cover design by: Art Painter
Library of Congress Control Number: 2018675309
Printed in the United States of America

CONTENTS

CHAPTER 1

Jayne poured herself another glass of wine.

Looking out across the bay in the soft evening light she could see the castle on top of the steep-sided hill rising out of the sea like something from a fairy tale. Its tall stone walls were almost growing out of the rocky mount it sat upon. The waves lapped around the base of the island, marooning the castle and its inhabitants out in the shallow sea of the curved bay.

She scribbled down her description in her new writer's notebook, purchased especially for this holiday. After a couple of lines her pen stopped moving.

She chewed on the end of it, then pulled it out of her mouth. This pen had cost a lot. She didn't want a leaky old biro, not when she was Becoming a Writer.

She smiled at herself, wondering why she always thought of that phrase with capital letters. Perhaps it was because it had been her secret dream for so long. And now she was actually doing it. She was alone, unencumbered, and free to 'Become a Writer,' even if it really wasn't in the way she'd hoped.

But it wasn't turning out to be as easy as she'd expected. Maybe she should have a go at her knitting instead, just until she got some more writerly ideas.

She took another hearty sip of the wine, more of a gulp, if she was honest. It really was very good. It had cost over ten pounds a bottle. Perhaps it would stimulate her senses and allow the words to flow.

It really was lovely, sitting by the open window.

'You'll catch your death,' Derek would have said, ushering her away from the supposedly deadly breeze. But only one of them was dead, so...

Jayne took another sip. Another pound—or was a small sip only fifty pence? Derek would have known. He always knew the price of everything and counted the cost of whatever they did. She missed that now.

She stared down at her few lines on her page and then back up at the view from her window.

Come on, surely she could write a longer description of the view? It was exceptional. There was an ancient castle on a tiny island out in the bay, surrounded by sea and the stars above.

It wasn't something she would ever see out of her window in Hertfordshire. And yet she'd run out steam already.

She drew a squiggly line under her writing and added in brackets, '*Fill in the description later.*'

Then she looked back at her notebook. Did real writers do that? Or could they always be bothered to fill in the descriptions?

This setting was the perfect backdrop to the romance she was determined to write. She'd rented the apartment overlooking the sea for a month, and that should be long enough to write something and kick-start her new life as a romantic novelist. To 'Become a Writer.'

At least the view took her eyes off the rest of the accommodation. The apartment itself was rather disappointing. It didn't look much like the pictures. The advertisement had shown a clean, light, bright space with a pale blue sofa and a nice big pot plant. But her sofa was a chintzy, gaudy pink, and there wasn't even a dried-up old cactus in the room.

Jayne had half a mind to call the holiday company and speak to them. But what would they do now? She knew the whole village got booked up in summer.

And of course, she had been allowed her to bring Toby

with her. So many of them didn't allow dogs, but there was no way she was coming away for a whole month without Toby.

She stared out at the sea as night fell. '*Night lowered its dim shroud over the castle,*' she wrote in her notebook, momentarily pleased with herself. Then she frowned. No, that wouldn't do at all. A shroud was something that people were buried in. Her descriptions should be full of references to silk and bodices and ribbons and so on, not death shrouds.

Perhaps she should abandon the writing for tonight and carry on with her knitting. That didn't take as much thinking about, not once she got going.

The window of the apartment next door opened with a noisy creak.

Another admirer of the view, she guessed. But then she heard a match strike and the pungent odour of pipe tobacco wafted across in front of her.

She coughed, trying to hide the sound in case it came across as a little pointed, too deliberate.

But the smoke caught in her throat, and she couldn't help coughing again, louder this time.

"All right, all right, Missus, don't get your knickers in a twist," came a surly voice out of the darkness.

She froze. Was this man talking to her? Should she apologise? But she still couldn't speak. It was all she could do to not cough again.

She inched back from the window and tried to pull it closed as quietly as she could.

Perhaps she'd go outside and sit on the wall by the beach.

Toby could do with his nightly ablutions. She would take her notebook, just in case the muse struck. *The sky is like a sheet of silk.* Not a shroud. Now that was much better.

Why hadn't she thought of that the first time?

She crossed out the line with 'shroud' in it and scribbled

down 'silk' in her notebook before she put Toby's lead on and slipped on her comfortable shoes.

Toby wagged his tail, as enthusiastic about life as ever, and she led him out of the apartment, past the door of the grumpy smoker, and down two flights of stairs. There were at least ten apartments here. Were they all rented out to summer tourists? Mr. Grumpy didn't seem like he was in a holiday mood.

She pushed open the heavy outer door and stepped into the narrow main street. The village had several pubs and a few shops all clustered behind the lovely half-moon of the beach. It was perfect.

She was going to head left, down to the central square and through it to the main beach access. But Toby was determined to go the other way.

He was following a very interesting scent, his tail wagging and his claws scrabbling at the pavement. He resisted all her attempts to pull him in the other direction.

She sighed and gave in. She knew better than to try and change her dog's mind. He was a small white and brown Jack Russell terrier, and the breed was known for being wilful. They were loyal and friendly and deeply affectionate, but definitely stubborn. When it came to a battle of wills, he always won out.

She let him lead her slightly uphill and then to the right, down through a narrow lane of houses and back toward the sea.

Her eyes became more accustomed to the dark and she decided it looked charming. Perhaps these were the old fisherman's cottages. Maybe her romantic hero could live in one of them. He would be a tall and weather-beaten man of the ocean, with warm brown eyes.

She let Toby pull her along as her mind wandered, filled with thoughts of the fisherman. But would he do as a romantic hero? If he was a fisherman, would he smell of fish? Perhaps she could have him washing his hands and showering regularly... But he would come across as having an obsession with cleanliness and that wasn't ideal for her novel either.

She sighed. It was difficult to conjure a perfect hero. But she was convinced that a few weeks here in this beautiful corner of Cornwall would soon get her inspiration flowing.

The cottages petered out and the lane became a path, and she was at the coast again. The pathway ran along the top of a low makeshift wall with the scrap of sand below and a small jetty up ahead.

This wasn't the big main beach, the proper stretch of wide sand where all the tourists went. This was the other end of the village with just a thin, narrow stretch of rocks and sand, hidden out of the way. Perhaps it was better for Toby.

Toby followed the grass at the top of the slope, staying off the beach itself. Good. She didn't really want sand in her shoes at this time of night.

She padded along the path at the top of the beach.

We mustn't go too far, she decided. It was getting darker by the minute. The few lights from the houses had gone and she could barely see where she was going.

She didn't want to get lost in the dark or fall down a hole on the very first night of her holiday.

Jayne heard something below. Was that the sound of feet crunching on the gravelly sand? She could hear voices too.

She peered into the darkness. She could just see the outlines of people in the shadowy darkness. They were talking in low voices, not very far away from her.

Oh dear. Perhaps this wasn't safe—a woman walking alone at night? Maybe she should head back now. But Toby chose that very moment to do his business, finding a suitable spot and circling for a few minutes before committing to it.

She stood there awkwardly as Toby did what he needed to. The dark shapes moved along the beach below her, toward the little jetty.

"We'll just do it. Get it over with. Tonight." The voice was deep and soft.

"The tides aren't right." This voice was a little higher, more anxious perhaps but with that charming West Country accent. 'Toids' not 'tides.' 'Roight' not right.

When she wrote her novel, would she write out the fisherman's charming accent like that? She could try to do it phonetically. Or would that just get terribly tiresome—or even come across as patronising? It was a tricky, writerly decision, the sort she had to wrestle with now, she thought happily.

"Damn the tides. Once he's in, he's in." Back to Mr. Deep and Soft.

Whoever they were, they seemed very intent on something. Perhaps fishing was a more contentious business than she'd realised.

Maybe her handsome romantic hero would have a troubled soul because of the difficulties of fishing and the awkwardness of the tides. Her heroine could soothe him. *'You'll catch more fish, my love, I know you will.'* She would believe in him and the power of his nets and his ability to read the tides. The 'toids.'

Toby finished his business and now came the unpleasant side of dog ownership—picking up after him. The job done and her baggy swinging by her side, she turned to leave.

Those people seemed to have disappeared into the darkness.

She headed back to her apartment, wondering if the grumpy man would still be smoking near her window, and where there was an outside bin for Toby's little contribution.

Perhaps paradise wasn't going to be quite as perfect as she'd hoped.

CHAPTER 2

The next morning, Jayne had a mild hangover. A whole bottle of red wine to herself was more than she was accustomed to.

Toby didn't care. His front paws were on the bed and his face, white with a light brown patch over one eye, was already looking at her, eager and ready to go.

As she stirred and sat up, he cocked his head to the side, as if he was saying, 'Well, come on. I can't wait forever.'

Derek had been an early riser and he'd got Toby accustomed to an early morning excursion and she couldn't seem to get the little dog out of his habit.

She groaned and rolled heavily out of bed. Early mornings were not her forte, and yet she knew she would get no rest until Toby had been out.

She pulled on a baggy sweatshirt, and loose jogging bottoms. There was no need for a bra. She didn't wash her face, just smoothed her hair down and yawned widely.

With any luck, the streets would be as deserted as they were in Hertfordshire at this time of day.

The only people she ever saw on her early morning walks at home were the commuters—the smartly dressed men and women, with their heads down marching to the train station to mine the money pits of London.

They never even glanced at a sleep-addled woman strolling slowly down the street with a dog. It would be the same here, no doubt.

She pulled her shoes on, and half-stumbled down the stairs with Toby pulling on his leash and eagerly leading the way.

He insisted on the same path as last night.

In the early morning sunlight, it looked even prettier, even if the light was hurting her eyes. She resolved to stop drinking when she'd had half a bottle next time.

Jayne squinted at her surroundings through half-closed eyes. There were the small, higgledy-piggledy, white-washed cottages, built right up to the side of the road, and the glorious sea was just at the bottom of the narrow lane.

She ambled down the lane, letting Toby's leash out to the fullest extent so he could sniff and dash around wherever he wanted.

Jayne wished she'd had some coffee, or at least a glass of water. Toby's insistence on early-morning walks wasn't her favourite thing about him. But the dog had kept her going after Derek passed. Toby was her only reason to get up in the morning, and there was always the need to go out for a walk. Getting up and getting out of the house were simple things, but they'd got her through the darkest days.

Now, look at this! She paused for a moment, admiring it.

It was just the prettiest little cottage, with four low windows, their light blue paint peeling slightly, and a matching blue painted door. A terracotta pot of golden yellow marigolds flowered brightly at the entrance. The faded sign read, 'Endon Cottage.'

"This is perfect, isn't it Toby? My hero can live here. It's the sweetest, most romantic little place. What do you think, Toby? Is it suitable for my rather windswept hero, the delightful if rather odorous fisherman? Or shall we make him a sea captain? Would that be less fishy?"

Toby didn't answer. He was much more of a do-er than a talker and he just gave her a wag of the tail that she took as agreement and pulled on the leash.

"What do you want with him?"

The voice startled her and Jayne gave a little yelp of shock.

Turning, she saw a woman in the doorway of the adjoining cottage. This cottage was almost as pretty. It was smooth whitewashed stone, with thick walls, a light green wooden door, shutters at the windows and a pot of delightful, tropical-looking flowers by the door.

The woman was sturdy with long red-hair flapping in the wind and a face that was bravely meeting the world bare and scrubbed, untroubled by powders or creams to soften the wrinkles at the corners of her eyes.

She had sharp hazel eyes and was staring right at Jayne with a somewhat confrontational air. "What do you want with him?" the woman repeated, her tone even more brusque.

"Oh, er, I was just admiring the cottage. It's so lovely here," Jayne said, trying to be nice.

The woman shook her head as if she didn't believe Jayne. "Oh. Really? So you're not looking for *him*?" She cocked her head at the house next to hers. "You wouldn't be the first woman turning up here, trying to pin him down. Well, he's not here. So you can go."

Jayne "No, no. I'm not looking for anyone. I'm just passing." What was this woman talking about? And why did she seem so irritated?

Jayne continued explaining herself. "I'm just taking the dog out, you know. He likes it down here. He…" Well, she couldn't explain that once Toby had found a spot to do his business, he liked to return there regularly. No. That was altogether too much information for anyone, especially at this time of the morning.

"They are just lovely flowers. What are they?" Jayne gestured to the large pot by the woman's doorway, making an abrupt change of subject, hoping to get the woman away from her accusations of… Of what? Looking for someone who lived next door to her?

It was a pot full of a rather elegant, tall woody-stemmed plant with big white trumpet-shaped flowers hanging down.

"Angel's Trumpets," the woman said, still not altogether mollified.

Jayne reached down and lifted the head of a flower.

"Don't touch," the woman snapped.

She really wasn't very friendly at all.

"Well, they are lovely," Jayne repeated. She didn't look the woman in the eye. It wasn't only because of the woman's unfriendly glare, but Jayne knew that she herself wasn't exactly looking her best.

She really wasn't up to any kind of interaction, let alone this rather unfriendly one, not before at least two cups of coffee and tidying herself up.

So much for thinking the red-headed woman could do with a few touches of make-up and moisturiser—Jayne knew she could do with the same herself.

But all the same, Jayne found herself wondering if this woman would suffice as the model for her romantic heroine?

Perhaps she had lived next door to the handsome sea captain all her life and harboured a secret crush on him, but he'd never noticed her until something happened... Maybe she saved his life or did something dramatic.

Jayne cast another glance at the woman. She was still glaring at Jayne. And no, she looked far too challenging and her shoulders were very wide for a romantic heroine and her voice was slightly deep and very assertive.

No, she wouldn't suit a bodice at all, and she certainly didn't look as though she would ever be swept off her feet by a dashing hero. Instead of whispering sweet nothings, she was more likely to ask him what on earth he thought he was doing and hit him over the head with a rolling pin.

Anyway, luckily, the woman had lost interest in Jayne and gone back into her little cottage, leaving her door half-open, no doubt ready to spring out on the next hapless passer-by and demand to know their reason for being here.

Not the pleasantest of women to meet at any time, Jayne thought, wondering if a lot of the locals would be like this. She'd already had Mr. Grumpy grumbling at her last night, and now this woman was annoyed by Jayne's mere presence.

So much for a sweet little village full of charming and friendly locals, she thought glumly.

Jayne continued down, led by Toby, wondering if it would be this spot for his ablutions for the rest of her stay. He liked a routine. But she rather hoped she wouldn't have to see the angry red-headed woman every day.

The narrow stretch of beach was completely deserted. The waves lapped gently at the shore, and she gazed happily out at St Michael's Mount, the little island in the bay, with its beautiful castle, rising up out of the water.

The view made up for everything. So, the inhabitants might not be welcoming her with open arms, but she didn't care, not really. The place itself was perfect.

If she couldn't come up with a romantic tale set here in this magical spot, then she had no hope of ever 'Becoming a Writer.'

Toby pulled on his lead, seemingly determined to get down onto the beach today.

Could she be bothered to climb down there?

Toby pulled again, determined.

Jayne gave in and lowered herself down on the wall, sat there for a moment and then dropped down rather heavily onto the sand, with an unladylike groan, rather like those tennis players.

Perhaps this holiday would kick-start her fitness

programme too. A romantic novelist, fit and healthy. It might be the start of a whole new era.

She shook her feet, but they sank into the sand again, the grit determined to get right inside her shoes.

Toby tugged her along the sand, snuffling here and there excitedly.

He wasn't used to the beach. Neither was she. Despite the sunshine, the wind coming off the sea was actually quite cold and she could feel her nose going red and her hair was flapping wildly against her head and face.

She leaned down and let Toby off his leash and dug in her pocket for a tissue to dab at her nose and tried to smooth her hair down again, but it was no good, not in this wind.

Toby ran around excitedly for a while, dashing at the seagulls and scratching earnestly at random patches of sand.

She leaned against the wall, keeping half an eye on him, hoping he'd do what he needed to do soon so she could get back and put the coffee on to brew.

Toby had caught a scent and snuffled along, his nose down and his tail up, wagging like a beacon.

He rushed along to the small stone jetty and began to bark, his sharp yips of alarm sounding even louder in the early morning silence.

"Toby. Hush," she called, completely ineffectually.

Trying to stop a Jack Russell from barking was almost impossible, and if there was a knack to it she certainly hadn't mastered it in Toby's five years. They were very vocal dogs and Toby was no exception.

Jayne hurried along the beach, trying to catch up to him. It wasn't easy to walk on the sand. Her feet were sinking at every step. "Toby, no. Toby, quiet," she called out, but he didn't take any notice of her.

The only way to stop him was to put his leash back on and

pull him away and distract him from his barking.

She caught up with Toby, nosing at a pile of clothes piled against the base of the jetty.

Then she looked again, taking it in properly, shock making her rigid.

"Hello. Are you all right? Er—hello?" she said, her voice getting louder, joining the insistent barking of her dog.

She leaned down and touched the man, shaking his shoulder, but she knew.

She knew he wasn't all right.

She knew he wasn't going to answer her.

He wasn't ever going to answer anyone again.

CHAPTER 3

Jayne's heart was pounding and she wondered if she was going to be ill.

She fumbled for her phone. There was no signal.

She looked around wildly, but there was not a soul in sight.

She was on a beach in a strange place, with a dead man and a dog that wouldn't stop barking. What should she do?

Panic rose in her and she felt herself starting to crumble a little.

The man's face was white, a horrible pale shade of bluey white. His eyes were open and staring upwards but cloudy-looking, unseeing. His shoulder had been ice-cold and wet when she'd touched him.

She wished she hadn't looked at him and she especially wished she hadn't touched him. But she had.

She took a breath, reflexively clutching at the locket around her neck. It held a photo of her anda picture of her husband. She heard Derek's voice in her head. 'You can deal with this, Jayne. Calm down. It's okay. You can do it.'

She breathed deeply.

What should she do? Stay with the deceased, try CPR if there was any probability of it being of any use, and call 999.

But there was no need for CPR. The man was cold and blue and she knew instinctively that he was way beyond that kind of help. But she needed to get someone. Calling an ambulance or the police wasn't easy when there was no mobile phone signal.

She turned on her heel and marched back the way she came. Her feet sank into the sand as if it was trying to slow her down and keep her there with the dead man.

She struggled along the beach, up onto the wall and back into the lane. For once, Toby was being helpful and was running along at her heel. She clipped his leash back on. "Come on, boy. I know who can help," she said to him.

In a few moments, she was banging on the half-open door of the big-shouldered, red-headed woman.

The woman appeared in the hallway. "What is it now? I told you. He's not here," she snapped.

Jayne shook her head, her chest heaving, gasping with breathlessness from her rushing and from shock. "Call the police. There's a body on the beach. A man. He's dead."

"Oh." The red-headed woman stared at her for a long moment. "Right. I suppose you had better come in."

The woman checked up and down the street. Perhaps she was hoping there would be someone else around that she could foist Jayne onto, but it was deserted.

Jayne found herself hustled into the little cottage, and sitting at a small pine kitchen table.

"A body? A dead body? Of a man, you said? Are you *sure*?" the woman asked.

"Yes. Yes," Jayne replied, hardly able to believe it herself. "Please, phone the police. I've got no signal." She waved her mobile at the woman.

"Yes. I'll call them. Now, you sit down. You look like you've had a terrible shock." She sounded almost friendly now, her earlier irritation changed for a honeyed sweetness in her voice.

In just a few moments, the woman handed Jayne a mug of warm tea. It had plenty of milk and sugar in it too.

"Drink this. It will help with the shock."

Jayne sipped it gratefully. She didn't usually take sugar, but perhaps she needed it now, after what she'd seen.

"I'll go and phone the police now," the woman said. "You just sit there and drink that. You've had a nasty shock, haven't you?"

Jayne nodded, trying to gather her thoughts. Toby sat beside her and she put down her tea and stroked his head, soothing herself as much as him.

She heard the woman making a phone call, a low murmur from behind the door. There was a long pause and then more talking.

Jayne sipped the tea, Toby sitting close to her legs as if he wasn't sure about this strange turn his morning walk had taken at all.

The woman came back into the room. "There. Now, someone will be along soon. Do you want another cup of tea? And then you'd better tell me about it. I'm Kensa, by the way."

Her hands still shaking, Jayne told Kensa what had happened, trying not to embellish it with any fanciful details.

"I thought it was a bundle of clothes at first. And then, I took a single step closer and oh! The horror! I was looking straight into cold, dead eyes."

Kensa looked at her quizzically. "Oh, the horror indeed. What did he look like?"

"Like a dead man," Jayne whispered, clutching her cup and drinking some more.

"Yes, but like an old dead man or young dead man? Was he bald? What colour hair did he have? I mean, what did he actually look like, apart from dead?"

Jayne knew she was getting carried away with the drama of the moment.

She was the heroine now — bravely making a terrible discovery and seeking for help. She was the central character, all of a sudden. Maybe in her story her heroine would find a body, and weep piteously over it for hours...

"Jane, is it? Did you say your name was Jane?"

"Mm. Jayne. With a y. Jayne."

"Well, Jayne, you don't seem to remember much about what you saw."

"All I can remember is his eyes, staring blankly up to the heavens, never to see anything again."

Kensa looked at her oddly. "Well, that's that then."

"How long will it be until the police arrive? Or will they send an ambulance? Or both, perhaps?" Jayne had no idea how these things worked.

Kensa shrugged. "Police, I guess. Most likely."

"It's been ages since you rang."

Kensa checked her phone. "About twenty minutes, I suppose. Not too bad. They'll be coming from Penzance. It takes quite a while. I'll have a look up the lane. If they miss the turning, they'll have to go right out to the other end of town before they can turn round. Most people miss the turning."

As if on cue, Kensa's phone rang.

"Is it the police?" Jayne asked, squinting at the screen. But the incoming call was flashing 'Dave.'

Kensa checked the screen and shook her head. "I'll get this and go and keep an eye out for the police."

She bustled off, heading up the lane, phone in hand.

Jayne looked at her own phone. She had a tiny signal, but not enough to call anyone. And there was no need. The police were on their way, and she just had to sit and wait.

Jayne looked around the kitchen. It was quaint and old fashioned, with a scrubbed pine table and two chairs, and a pile of dirty dishes near the sink. There were actually a lot of used dishes and dirty glasses for one woman. Perhaps she had a whole family living here. Pots stood on the stove, three of them, each

17

with some congealed mass or thick liquid in the bottom.

Kensa clearly didn't care to wash up until she'd run out of everything.

Jayne inspected her own mug. It didn't look too clean either, with dark tannin stains around the inside, and it tasted a little odd. An open carton of milk stood out on the side. It could be on the turn if the woman, Kensa, didn't keep it in the fridge.

Jayne was sure she could smell something. Was it the milk going sour or one of those concoctions on the stove?

She sighed. She was hot now that she was out of the wind and after she had run up the beach. Her face was red, and her hair was salty and untameable. She wished again she'd taken a little more care to dress properly. She wasn't even wearing underwear, so she didn't want to take her jacket off and cool down. Of course, she hadn't expected to actually see anyone, except perhaps in passing.

She rubbed her hot, damp face. A clump of mascara from yesterday stuck to her fingers. She really must look a fright, especially crying and wailing as she had been. Like a woman possessed.

She stared around the little cottage wondering what it would be like to live in such a cosy little space, right next to the sea.

The kitchen was old and tired, and she could see through the half-open door to the lounge area. It looked cramped too, with a coffee table covered in letters and colourful rolls of paper and what looked like estate agent's brochures.

Jayne considered living in a cottage like this. She could sell her big family house up in Hertfordshire, and get somewhere smaller, somewhere like this, but clean and tidy and nicely decorated. It could be a new project. She had been advised not to make any major decisions after her bereavement. That would probably count as a major decision.

Still, it was nice to think about. If she moved here, or

somewhere like it, she'd choose a pale blue and off-white colour scheme, with accents of yellow. A few nice plants, a stylish chair or two, and a much more minimalist look, she decided.

Her mind drifted as she mentally redecorated the kitchen and the lounge, wondering if she could be happy in a little cottage like this. It would be a new start.

But she wouldn't be too happy if dead men kept turning up not far from the bottom of the garden.

In her novel, the one she was just about to start writing, her heroine would live somewhere like this, although she wouldn't be modelled on the rather burly Kensa, and her heroine would definitely tidy up once in a while. Unlike Kensa.

And where *was* Kensa? She'd been gone for far too long. Jayne started to panic, wondering if something awful had happened to her too. Was there a killer on the loose in this quaint little village?

CHAPTER 4

Trying to distract herself, Jayne stood up and rinsed her mug, and then picked up a cloth and gave it a proper wipe. With a bit of determination, she managed to get out all the tannin stains and rinsed away the rather sticky tea leaves at the bottom.

'I don't know what kind of tea she's using, but I don't like it much,' Jayne thought. 'Well, at least the woman's got one clean mug now.'

She set it down next to the sink, hoping it would act as a hint to Kensa to give the rest of the crockery and glassware a proper wash.

Then she waited. Where was Kensa? Should she go and look for her—and risk meeting the killer, if there was one?

'Calm down, Jayne, everything will be fine,' she heard Derek say. It was almost as if he was in the room with her. Jayne looked around, just checking, even though she knew she was being ridiculous.

A noise startled her, and she stood up again, knocking her chair over and making herself jump all over again.

With a sigh of relief, Jayne saw that it was Kensa coming back, followed by a single, young-looking policeman.

Jayne had expected a whole team of police and detectives and the coroner or was it a pathologist? Which one was it that examined the body and usually found the clue that solved the crime? She couldn't remember now, but she knew was some kind of scientist—and usually a very attractive woman, if the television was to be believed.

Perhaps the rest of the team were following, or they'd already gone directly to the beach.

"Are you alright?" Kensa asked. "What are you doing?"

Jayne realised she was standing up, her chair overturned behind her, one hand gripping Toby's leash tightly, ready to run from serial killers or ghosts, even if it was the kindly ghost of her husband.

"Oh, I just… I heard a noise. But it's you. I thought it was…" She stopped there. She wasn't going to admit she had thought—for one silly second—that it actually was the ghost of her dead husband in the room with her. The shock had evidently made her more susceptible and nervous than she'd thought.

The policeman looked her up and down and then took a seat opposite her.

His pale, narrow face had a bad dose of acne, the poor thing, and somehow, he didn't inspire any confidence in her.

"Why don't you sit down?" he suggested, gesturing to her chair. "I'm Officer Jefferies. And you are?"

"Jayne. With a y. J-A-Y-N-E. Jayne Jewell. I'm on holiday here."

"Right." He wrote her name down and then added, 'on holiday,' afterwards. He was diligent, she thought.

Kensa stood at the sink, finally washing up, starting with the saucepans on the stove.

She should do the glasses first, Jayne thought, but she could hardly break off her police interview to advise another woman to wash the glasses while the water was still clean, then move onto the dirtier things.

"Address?"

She spelled it out, giving him both her home address in Hertfordshire and her temporary address in the village.

He was a slow writer, taking his time over the capitals and punctuation.

He's careful, I suppose, Jayne thought, her impatience growing as he laboriously added the postcode for her holiday address. Why did he need that? It wasn't as if they were going to be pen pals.

Finally, they got to the point of the visit.

"I believe you saw something on the beach?"

"A body. Of a man. Staring blankly up at the heavens."

"A body. Of a man. Staring blankly up at the heavens," he repeated as he noted it down.

He was writing every word down. This could take forever.

"And where was this?"

"On the beach. By the jetty. I can show you, now, if you like?"

"Are you sure you feel up to it? You can stay here and have a rest. I can go and look."

She guessed he was just being kind and trying to spare her from seeing that awful sight again. But his tone was quite condescending too, as if she was too weak to deal with it.

"No. I'm fine. I'll show you," she said, firmly.

"Right-o. Let's go and have a little look at what you say you saw, shall we?"

Jayne suppressed her irritation at his tone and led the way, with Toby following her.

It wasn't far—not as far as it had felt when she was struggling to get back up here with her heart pounding, all panicking and frantic.

"I couldn't get any signal on my phone down here, otherwise I'd have stayed with the body," she explained, trying to indicate that she knew the correct police procedure. After all, she had watched enough crime dramas on television.

Officer Jefferies nodded. "It's a mobile dead zone. It's a nightmare. It's the same where I live. I can't get a signal. Nothing at all."

He followed her along the beach.

She squinted into the early-morning light.

Where was it? Surely it should be obvious by now?

There had been a large black shape against the jetty, the clothes flapping.

A big old bundle of darkness.

But she couldn't see it now. The jetty wall looked clear.

She got closer and pointed. "It was here."

She stopped and turned around, checking her location. She'd not gone wrong, had she?

There weren't two jetties, or one off in a different direction?

No. This was it—it was exactly here.

But it wasn't here.

The body. It wasn't here.

Confused, she turned around again, looking in every direction.

The Police Officer and Kensa shared a look. It was a look that said they had never really expected to see a body. A look that said she was just a crazy woman.

That made Jayne even more insistent.

"It was *here*." She pointed insistently. "Right here. Look— you can see the marks in the sand. It's all upturned. There are drag marks and footprints."

The policeman bent down and looked closely.

Kensa said, "The fishermen go out from here every tide. There's bound to be a bit of disturbance in the sand."

"There you go," Officer Jefferies said, as if that explained it. He straightened up again. "And look at your dog, messing it up too."

"But it was here!" Jayne looked around wildly again, and

then clambered onto the jetty, all too aware that her rear end was flailing around in a very ungainly way as she tried to climb up onto it. She tugged at Toby's leash. He was scrabbling in the sand, messing up all the drag marks she was sure she had seen. "Toby. Stop destroying the evidence," she called out. But he kept digging and scattering sand everywhere.

The Policeman jumped up next to her, annoyingly limber.

He looked with her over the other side of the jetty. There was nothing there. Nobody—and certainly no body.

"You're sure it was here and not on the other beach? Tourists such as yourself don't often come down this way. What were you doing here anyway?"

He looked at her with narrowed eyes, as if suddenly *she* was under suspicion.

"I was walking my dog. And it was here. I swear it was. It was. It really was. I saw it. I did."

Even she could hear that her voice sounded more anxious and desperate to be believed—and less convincing because of it.

Kensa watched them from a distance.

Officer Jefferies nodded slowly.

"More than likely, it was just some old fellow just taking a nap and now he's gone home."

"He was dead. He had cold, dead eyes," she repeated. Why wouldn't he believe her?

"Staring blankly up at the heavens. Yes," he said. "But he can't have been dead, can he? Otherwise, he wouldn't have gone away. He'd still be here."

"Unless someone moved him," Jayne said excitedly. "Look, that must be what happened! Someone moved the body. You need to check the area properly—to search for clues. Look! I can see something."

A little piece of paper caught her eye.

She sat on the edge of the jetty and dropped down onto

the sand. It was further down than she expected, and she stumbled and fell to her knees.

Toby leapt at her, convinced she was playing a fun new game, and tried to lick her face. He pushed his sandy wet nose against her cheek.

But she scrabbled over the sand and grabbed the paper.

"You see! It's a clue!" She held it tight, afraid the wind would whip it away.

Toby barked in excitement and leapt at her again.

Kensa came and looked. "That's just a ferry ticket. For the boat across to the Mount. There are hundreds of these sold every day. It's not a clue. It's just litter." Her tone was dismissive, even slightly sneering, as if Jayne was a stupid outsider who didn't understand anything.

"But you need to check properly. Examine the scene, rope it off and sieve through the sand," Jayne said rather desperately as Officer Jefferies sauntered over.

"This isn't CSI Marazion. If there's no body, there's no investigation." He shrugged.

Jayne felt the air go out of her. She *had* seen a body. She had. And yet these two were looking at each other as if they were in the presence of a crazy lady.

"Well, I'll stay and have a wander around, but you two can go back home now. Thank you for your help, but it doesn't look like there's much to worry about here. Still, better safe than sorry, eh? Just maybe you should check a bit more before you call anything in again. I don't want to be racing over here every time you see some old fellow having a nap on the beach."

He and Kensa laughed, and he said something to her under his breath.

Jayne knew she didn't look very convincing, gripping her scrap of paper, her dog running everywhere and barking and now leaping at her and pushing sand into her face, her hair flapping everywhere, her hands shaking with the shock of it all.

She got to her feet and trudged back up the beach.

She'd barely been here for forty-eight hours, and she'd made a fool of herself already.

But then she shook her head and looked down at Toby.

He'd seen it too. He'd been barking and pawing at it. He knew that man wasn't sleeping.

She *had* seen it, and it had been awful.

And the body had disappeared, even if they didn't believe her.

Sooner or later, she'd be proved right, she was sure of it.

CHAPTER 5

Jayne walked back to her apartment feeling upset and deflated.

On her way back, she passed the pasty shop, Trelawney's. A heavenly aroma of savoury baking permeated the air.

She paused by the door—well, why not, after the morning she'd had?

Jayne went into the shop, drawn in by the wonderful smell.

A woman came through from the back, summoned by the bell that jangled when the door opened. She was a thin woman with a pale face and wisps of brown hair escaping from her hairnet. "Oh, no. Not in here. Get out!" the woman exclaimed.

Jayne stepped back, shocked. Another person snapping at her! Why was everyone so unpleasant around here?

"Not you. I mean the dog. We can't have dogs in here," the woman said.

Jayne looked down at Toby. She'd not even been aware of bringing him in. Of course, he wasn't allowed in a bakery.

"I'm so sorry. I'm a bit all over the place," Jayne apologised, backing out of the door. This really had been a very difficult morning.

"There's a hook outside," the women called, perhaps trying to make amends for her initial sharpness of tone.

Jayne looped Toby's leash around the hook and went back in. To her embarrassment, she felt her face flushing and tears springing up in her eyes.

She leaned on the counter for support, trying to get a grip.

One hand on her locket, she listened for Derek's calm, reassuring voice, but all she could hear was the woman, talking about pasties.

"You're early. The pasties will still be a couple of minutes, if you don't mind waiting. Small? Medium? Large? Only the steak ones will be ready. The veggie ones don't go on until later."

"That's fine. Whatever you've got. And medium please," Jayne said. Her voice came out a bit tense and tight.

"Are you alright? You look a bit..." The woman stopped talking.

"I'm fine," Jayne said. "It's just been a difficult morning."

"Oh! That was you with the policeman! I saw the car going past, and then turning down the lane. Then after, I saw you and the officer walking down towards the beach. Has something happened? Are you alright?" the woman asked again, obviously determined to get to the bottom of it.

Jayne knew she couldn't deny all knowledge of it, not if she'd been seen with Officer Jefferies. "I thought I saw something on the beach, so I called the police but it must have been a mistake." She felt silly even saying it.

The woman stared at her. "You called the police? Why? What did you see on the beach to get the police down there?"

"The mind can play tricks, I suppose," Jayne said. "I thought I saw a body actually. It sounds so stupid now, but at the time I really thought I saw it." She laughed, feeling a little embarrassed now. It did seem ridiculous, standing here in this cheerful bakery, saying she'd seen a dead body.

"Oh. What did the police say?"

"It had gone when we got back there. Just vanished. But maybe if you could see me and the police officer, you saw the body too, from the window?" Hope flared in Jayne. Perhaps this woman could corroborate her story and stop her feeling so stupid.

The woman shrugged. "I can only see the lane and who comes and goes down there. I can't see the beach. Anyway, I wasn't taking much notice. But if it upped and went, it can't have been a body, can it?"

"That's what the police said," Jayne said glumly, her hopes dashed. "But maybe you saw *something* useful from your window? Shall I tell the police?" Even if she hadn't seen the body, she might have noticed shady characters going up and down the lane.

"No. Don't say anything. I can't see that much from the window. It's not like I was watching," the woman added defensively.

A man came out of the back of the shop with a baker's apron on. "Everything alright, Mary?" he asked.

Mary frowned at Jayne and gave a little shake of her head, as if to say, 'don't say anything else about it.'

"Yes. Fine. I'll go and see if the pasties are ready. It was a medium steak, wasn't it?"

They both went back into the rear of the shop.

Looking in, Jayne could see big ovens, long tables covered in flour and racks ready to hold the baked goods. They made everything fresh here on the premises. No wonder the village was always full of the delicious smells of baking.

A few minutes later the waif-like woman, Mary, was back, with a huge pasty poking out from a paper bag.

"Oh, I wanted a medium," Jayne said.

"That is a medium." She passed it over.

"But it's huge. And hot!" Jayne added, juggling it from hand to hand.

"It's fresh out of the oven. I told you they were only just ready. That one's on the house. Especially for you. You look like you've had a hard morning."

Jayne smiled gratefully. "Thank you so much. How kind! I have had a difficult start to the day. I really have."

The woman frowned and touched her finger to her lips, as if to hush Jayne.

She got the message. "Thanks for this." It was nice to be treated with kindness. What with the young Police Officer who'd been condescending and Kensa's begrudging help and snappish manner, it had been less than pleasant.

But at least this woman, Mary, was kind and friendly.

Maybe it was a lovely place, Jayne thought, then remembered the horrible sight she'd seen earlier. "Thanks again. Bye," she called over her shoulder.

She unhooked Toby's leash from the post outside the shop and they hurried home.

Once she was back in the safety of the apartment, Jayne looked out of the window with a rather different set of glasses on —her rose-tinted ones were off and gloom-tinted ones were on.

Now, the castle on the island looked foreboding, its towering walls growing out of the granite as if it was trying to keep everyone out.

The sea was restless and the sound of the waves crashing against the rocks in the bay was relentless, powerful, almost frightening in its power.

She munched through the flaky pastry at one end of her pasty, and gradually the gloom began to lift a little.

However did anyone eat a whole one of these? It was endless—buttery pastry surrounding the rich goodness of the meat, vegetables inside all laced with hot black pepper.

She brewed a strong cup of coffee to wash it down.

She would need half a gallon to wash the whole pasty down.

All the while, Toby sat, very neatly just in front of her, his sharp brown eyes flicking from her face to the pasty and back again, until she gave up trying to eat the whole thing.

She broke what was left and put it in his dish.

Well, he was happy anyway.

And she felt better too. A pasty obviously had deeply restorative powers, as did her coffee.

She took out her writer's notebook, convinced she had to wrest something from the disaster of a morning so far.

She jotted down some details about the pretty cottages. Of course, her heroine would keep hers much tidier than Kensa did. But the white painted stone, the pale shutters, the scrubbed pine table—these would all make it into her story.

Jayne wrote for a few minutes, but every time she tried to think of her characters, the face of the dead man loomed into her mind.

She put down her pen and stared out of the window.

She had *definitely* seen a body. The sight would never leave her, she was certain of that.

Or was she going mad, as Kensa and the Police Officer clearly suspected? Jayne could recall his condescending manner, and their shared laughter at her insistence that she'd seen something. Neither of them believed her.

Tabitha, her daughter, sometimes hinted that Jayne was going senile. But that was more of a disapproving dig whenever Jayne did anything out of the ordinary—anything Tabitha didn't consider quite suitable for a 'woman of her age.'

Like when Jayne had started looking for holidays. The souks of Marrakech had beckoned—the winding alleys, the little shops, the exotic food, the beautiful riads, but Tabitha had said it was unsafe for a single woman, whatever her age.

Then Jayne had the idea of going to Rome or Florence, with their art and architecture and 'joie de vivre,' or was it 'La Dolce Vita,' for Italy?

Anyway, again, Tabitha insisted Jayne would be set upon by thieves and scoundrels, that there would be pickpockets on foot and on mopeds and all sorts of dangers and had said that it really wasn't wise for a woman 'at her time of life' to go.

Jayne had then suggested she might visit India. She knew Tabitha would hate the idea but Jayne had seen a lovely programme on television about a celebrity doing a tour of the temples and palaces and whatnot.

Tabitha had called her mad, asked her if she had a death wish, and hadn't she heard of *malaria*?

Then she had sat down with Jayne and looked at places online—ruling every single one a death-trap of some sort—until Jayne agreed to a month in Cornwall. In Marazion.

"And you can go from Paddington on the train and get a good discount with your railcard. You can't do that in India, now can you?" Tabitha had said, somewhat accusingly, as if India was deliberately trying to overcharge Jayne for rail travel.

Jayne didn't want to explain that, as far as she knew, India had a superb rail network.

"And Marazion is a lovely little town by the sea, with the beautiful St Michael's Mount in the bay. It's supposed to be quite lovely and it's very suitable for you, Mum. You can take your knitting. You enjoy knitting and you can have a nice relaxing time by the sea. Toby will enjoy too. Honestly, Mum, it's much better for you than going abroad."

Jayne stared out of her window. Tabitha was right. It was beautiful. It was stunning. And Toby loved it.

But *safe*? Well, would she have found a dead body—a *disappearing* dead body—in Marrakech or Rome or India?

She wanted to ring Tabitha and say 'I told you so' her, but she knew Tabitha would insist she immediately return to the safety of her leafy suburban home, or—even worse—Tabitha would show up here and 'keep an eye on her' until it wasn't a holiday at all.

Jayne suddenly began to feel more cheerful. She didn't need to call Tabitha, and she was going to stay here, despite the town's propensity for dead men on the beach.

And maybe, just maybe, she'd get to the bottom of what had happened.

She knew what she'd seen, and she knew that the man had been dead, and she knew that the body had somehow moved.

The ferry ticket might well have something to do with it, whatever Kensa said.

After all, not many tourists went on that side of the beach, and the ticket looked new. It wasn't a piece of old rubbish that had blown in days ago.

Something was definitely wrong in this pretty little village by the sea, and she wanted to find out what, if only for that poor man's sake.

But more than that, if she was honest, it was to be able to go and see that patronising young policeman and say a very satisfying, 'I told you so!' to him.

CHAPTER 6

"I think it's time for an excursion over to St. Michael's Mount," Jayne said, smiling down at Toby. Despite the awful start to the day, she was feeling full of energy.

"I know you don't like the sea much, but we'll check the tide times and see if we need to get a little ferry ticket of our own."

It wasn't what a police officer might call a lead, but it was all she had. And apart from anything else, it was about time she visited the magical-looking island in the bay.

She was quite excited by the prospect. Perhaps it was nervous energy. Whatever it was, she wanted to get out and about.

If she timed it right, she could walk across on the pathway through the sea—well, it wouldn't be *through* the sea, if she went at low tide.

When the tide was out, the island wasn't an island anymore and it looked easy to walk across on the broad stone pathway.

But at high tide, the water covered the pathway completely, the island was cut off and she'd already seen the small passenger boats going back and forth, shipping boat loads of tourists either way.

She got dressed properly, washed her face and brushed her hair and then packed her notebook in her rucksack. She might find some inspiration for a lovely scene for her romantic novel.

She took out her new jacket and backpack.

"Mum, you're going to Cornwall, not hiking in the Himalayas," Tabitha had said, slightly scornfully, when she saw Jayne's new purchases—the brightly coloured waterproof coat and the sturdy rucksack.

"It's Cornwall this time," Jayne had replied. "You never know where I'll go next time, now I don't have your father to look after. It might even be the Himalayas."

She was sure Tabitha had mumbled something about the next stop being an old people's home, but she chose to ignore it.

Poor Tabitha had taken Derek's passing hard. She was always a Daddy's girl, a careful, sensible child who had grown into a careful, sensible adult. But she was doing well for herself and seemed happy enough. Perhaps it was natural to try and protect her mother now, but it could be a bit much sometimes.

Jayne was sure new rucksack would come in handy today if she was climbing in and out of boats or traversing a pathway through the sea with Toby to take care of too.

"Come on, Tobes. Let's go and see what else this village has in store for us."

Toby seemed to nod wisely and followed her out.

Jayne walked briskly along the seafront, past the big hotel-pub that dominated the square. There must be lovely views from those rooms, she thought, wondering how much it was for a night. But they didn't take dogs. Not many places did.

Then she was at a slipway, which looked more like a paved road that sloped straight down into the waves.

The tide was in, lapping against the shore. So, she wasn't walking over there today.

She went to the small ticket office.

A few minutes later, she was substantially poorer, having paid for entrance to the Mount, and then another entrance fee to the gardens of the castle.

When she was asked for a third entrance fee to go into the castle itself, she baulked. The island and gardens were enough for one visit.

"When's the ferry?" Jayne asked.

The woman frowned. "We've only got one boat on today. We usually have two. So you'll have to wait for it to come back over, before you can go. Queue down there."

Jayne thanked her and led Toby down towards the slipway. She could see an open topped wide wooden boat in the distance, heading this way.

It was almost empty. Jayne checked her watch. It was still before ten am. Getting up early certainly helped to make the most of the day.

The boat arrived and a young woman jumped out and started checking people's tickets and issuing them with a boat ticket.

Jayne examined her ferry ticket carefully. It was a different colour to the one she had found on the beach. This was purple, printed on a long strip of cheap thick paper. The one she had for a clue was white.

She took it out of her pocket.

"Is this a ferry ticket too?" she asked.

The girl nodded. "But white is for Saturdays. Purple is for today. If you've not used that one, you can keep it until next Saturday if you want. But purple is today's colour."

Jayne nodded. That was helpful. It narrowed down when the ticket had been given out. Saturday. The day she arrived. The day before she saw the body.

The boat man took everyone's tickets, punching a little hole in the corner of each one and handing them back, and then helping people into the boat.

She put her ticket in one of her anorak's many pockets and zipped it up carefully. She'd need it for the boat back if the tide was still high.

She sat in the boat, right behind the boatman's seat. She tried to make Toby sit in the base of the boat, but there was water sloshing around and he didn't like that at all. He jumped up onto the bench seat next to her.

She tried to push him down, but he resisted, leaning all his weight against her, and she gave up. He could stay up there until the boat filled up. Maybe no one would need that seat. But she held his collar firmly.

The boat was rocking and dipping rather alarmingly. But she'd always had good sea legs and a strong stomach.

The boatman looked capable enough and the girl assisting seemed calm and cheerful. Clearly a little movement was to be expected and there was nothing to worry about.

More tourists arrived, a steady trickle of couples and families. Jayne was the only person travelling alone.

The boatman checked his watch. "Right, ten more minutes, see if we fill up. Sorry about the wait, but we've only got one boat running today," he announced.

His assistant sat by him. "Bloody Jay go, bloody useless," the young woman said in a low voice. "This is the third time this season he's not turned up."

"They should sack him. You could run a boat yourself now, girl."

She nodded. "I know. It's easy enough. I know the rocks and the routes and the tides. If it wasn't for bloody Jay go, I'd have my own boat by now. And at least I'd run it sober—and I wouldn't be skimming off the top. You'd think they would have noticed that the takings never match up."

Jayne listened idly to their conversation, glad she was sitting close enough to eavesdrop. Well, it wasn't eavesdropping really. After all, they could see her, sitting right there in her yellow and green waterproof jacket. She wasn't exactly sneaking around.

This Jay fellow was obviously not very popular. He was clearly unreliable and he was blocking this poor girl's promotion to independent boat person.

"But you'd miss his japes," the older man said, a smile cracking his craggy face. "Remember the time when he made that shark's fin and attached it to the boat. Halfway over to the Mount the tourists spotted it and started screaming. Shark attack! Shark attack!" He laughed to himself, wiping a tear from his eye as the mirth took him. "We almost lost a few over the side, there was so much panic in the boat."

The girl grinned too. "He should have been sacked for that as well. And that time he stopped next to the yacht and started speaking in French to them. He almost had them fooled that they'd sailed into France."

The girl laughed for a minute. "But I should still have my own boat," she said, returning to what was clearly a favourite theme.

The small dramas of village life, Jayne thought. But the boatman did sound amusing—as long as you weren't the one being terrified by the thought of a shark.

CHAPTER 7

Jayne watched the waves anxiously.

There weren't really sharks here, were there?

Even though the boat was still firmly moored up and there was no sign of any sea life at all, she didn't feel good. The swell was tipping the boat from side to side.

If she stared into the water, she could almost imagine a big shark lurking in the depths. She jumped slightly at a movement down in the deep and gripped the side more firmly.

The boat girl gave her an odd look. "We'll be setting off soon. Another five minutes," she said, as if Jayne was getting impatient rather than spooked by shadows.

A larger wave came and the boat rose up it, then dropped down the other side.

Some people laughed as sea-spray covered them in fine, cold salty drops, but Jayne was suddenly feeling queasy. She never got seasick. But the way this boat was going up and then down and then up and then down. Oh my.

And the sharks below. No. No sharks, she reminded herself. That had been a prank. A joke. But she couldn't get the idea out of her head.

She suddenly wished she hadn't got in at all. Perhaps she could get off, before they left. She really was feeling very nauseous and lightheaded. And there were sharks down there. She needed to get off.

But it was too late.

She leaned over the edge of the boat, clutching the side with one hand, the other still firmly on Toby's leash, and vomited profusely over the side.

She hung her head, feeling sweat prickle on her forehead and down her back.

More. There was more.

Her stomach rose and with a very unpleasant noise, she threw up again.

Toby whined and shoved his nose against her hand, clearly concerned. "Are you okay?" he seemed to ask, almost as if he was talking to her.

The boat girl turned and looked. "Do you want to get off? Not much of a sailor, hmm?" She spoke the words almost mechanically, as if vomiting ladies were ten-a-penny on this boat.

Jayne dragged her head up and pulled a tissue from her pocket and held it to her mouth, nodding.

"Yes, I need to get off. The sharks!" she whispered.

She knew everyone on the boat was looking at her. She could feel their glances—sympathy and amusement mixed.

They wouldn't be smiling if they knew there were sharks down there. Big ones with sharp teeth and staring eyes. Should she tell them?

She closed her eyes and dabbed her mouth again.

Looking over the side of the boat, she could have sworn she saw his face—the dead man's—looking up at her through the water, his cold, dead eyes fixed on hers, his teeth grinning, his mouth wide open like a shark's.

She cried out and then held the tissue against her mouth again. Was she going mad?

Standing up, Jayne allowed the girl to help her off the boat.

"Your ticket is good for the rest of the day. Or maybe you

should go over when the tide's out, so you can walk," the girl advised.

But Jayne was already staggering back up the slipway with Toby at her heels.

She saw a bench and sat down, glad to feel the sun on her face and solid earth under her feet. Was her stomach settled enough for her short walk home?

She still felt dizzy. The floor was moving, as if she was still on board the boat, and she could see the dead man just in the corner of her eye. But when she whipped her head around, there was nothing there. Just a litter bin, a few people walking, their faces turned towards the Mount. No one was looking at her, certainly not a dead man.

She got herself home and fell into bed. Toby took advantage and jumped up onto the bed and curled up next to her. She was too weak to shoo him off and dozed off with him tucked against her legs.

Hours later, she awoke, fiercely thirsty but more clear-headed and not nauseous anymore.

She sat up in bed, drinking her night-time glass of water.

How odd, to suddenly develop seasickness after a lifetime of being a good sailor.

She shook her head. Aging had its advantages, but it brought some unpleasant surprises too. Still, what was the alternative? Derek would never grow old, not now. She touched a finger to the locket, remembering the happier times when those photos had been taken.

She stood up abruptly. She'd learned to watch for maudlin thoughts creeping in. It was much better to keep busy, to keep moving. Get up and get on with something. It was the only way.

She cleaned herself up, showering and brushing her teeth again, and making sure her hair was tidy.

Yes, she'd had a horrible day so far—what with dead

bodies and patronising policemen and pasties that just wouldn't stay down.

But she was feeling much better now, and a cup of tea was definitely in order. She would have a nice relaxing afternoon, letting her stomach recover, and then she'd begin all over again tomorrow.

After all, she couldn't have two days in a row like this, could she?

Tomorrow was bound to be better.

She would devote herself to her writing this afternoon.

Jayne sat at the small table under the window and took out her notebook. It was going quite well. She had a few paragraphs down about the handsome sea captain, and the girl who lived next door who had a crush on him. Her sea captain was off on his voyages again and the girl was distraught.

'She looked at him with wide, violent eyes. "Please don't go," she begged.'

Jayne frowned at what she'd written. 'Violent eyes?' No. It should be violet eyes. That was what heroines had—although thinking about it, had she ever seen anyone with purple eyes? Perhaps violent was better—the girl could threaten him until he stayed. Maybe she would even do him in, and he would lie on the beach, dead and cold until a stranger found him. But that wasn't exactly a love story.

She sighed and put down her pen and looked at Toby. He gave a grumbling growl as if he was telling her to get on with it.

She still felt rather odd and not quite in control of her wandering thoughts.

She wanted to write a story where her characters at least stayed alive long enough to fall for each other.

Surely that was the least she could ask from a love story? But today's events had knocked all the romance out of her for now.

CHAPTER 8

Later that evening, her stomach quite settled now, she sat at the open window, gazing at the view. It hadn't lost its magic, not yet, even though she knew that out there, somewhere was a dead man.

She sighed. "I suppose there are dead people everywhere if you think about it," she said to Toby. "In hospitals and bedrooms, and by the side of the road. People die, and not always conveniently."

She was knitting instead of writing. The romance just wouldn't come today. Her heroine kept trying to kill off the hero, instead of swooning gracefully into his manly arms.

Her needles were clacking as she tried to ease the old rhythm back into her fingers. She hadn't knitted for a while now.

At one time, she could do it without even looking, but tonight she was checking the pattern and tensing the wool and counting her stitches.

She'd started knitting when Tabitha was a baby, and carried on through the years, but when Derek had become so ill and needed constant care, she'd stopped completely.

The way her thoughts roamed when she knitted wasn't safe. She needed a distraction that occupied her mind totally and didn't let her drift into the darkness. But now, perhaps she was alright to start again. It had been over a year since he'd passed, and she had her writing to focus on as well.

She knitted on, thinking about the romance and whether her hero and heroine would have an easy road to happiness.

No. Of course not. There would have to be some drama, some problems to overcome. But what should the impediment be? He didn't know she loved him. He was attracted to another woman who turned out to be all wrong for him or he was lost at sea and washed up on the beach, cold and grey and dead.

"No, not dead," she snapped to herself, refusing to allow her mind to dwell on that horrid image.

At the same time, a waft of blue pipe smoke announced that Mr Grumpy was back.

She sighed loudly in irritation.

The advertisement hadn't said the view would be wreathed in foul-smelling smoke for hours at a time. Not that it really was foul-smelling, once you got used to it. There was a fruity, earthy kind of undertone to it. Perhaps it was bearable.

"Caroline, is that you?" A head leaned out of the next-door window and loomed around, staring right in at her.

Rather alarmed to have her privacy so rudely breached, she pushed her chair back from the window and stood up. "No. It's me. Jayne. With a y."

He looked at her for a moment, as if he was making sure. "Oh. I heard the noise. And talking. You're knitting."

It sounded almost like an accusation. "Yes. Yes, I am," she said, with a hint of defiance. Surely she had a right to knit!

"Oh. That's what it was. I heard it and thought you were someone else. That's all."

The note of melancholy in his voice, and the way he turned away made her soften. She went closer to the window again, leaning out slightly and craned her head around to see him properly. He was a tall, gaunt man, puffing on his pipe.

"That's okay. Who did you think I was? Caroline, did you say?" she asked.

"Mm. The wife."

She smiled. "Well, I am definitely not your wife."

She stood back from the window again, put her knitting down carefully and reached for her notebook.

This had potential. If she was on a balcony and he was down below, it would be like something from Romeo and Juliet. *'No, Sir, I am not your wife!' the fair young maiden exclaimed, shocked at his suggestion.*

She scribbled hastily into her notebook, pleased with the scene she envisaged. A rather rakish gentleman, already married? A sweet but spirited young woman. Yes, this could be interesting.

"I've got a bottle of red open. If you want a glass."

She looked out of the window and peered around at him again, startled at his sudden change in tone. Was he actually being nice? Was he inviting her in?
"Uhm, I'm actually in my pyjamas." She certainly wasn't going to his apartment, even if it was just next door. He might seem—well, friendly was perhaps a going a little too far—unthreatening might be the best word. But all the same, she wasn't going to take any chances.

"No. I didn't mean that. You stay there and I'll pass you one through the window."

His head disappeared and a few seconds later, his arm reached out, a three-quarters full glass of wine in it. "There you go."

"Well, thank you." It was rather unorthodox but she could hardly say no. She took the glass, and put it carefully on her side table, next to her notebook.

Toby had his paws on the windowsill, his head straining out, a warning grumble in his throat. Jayne laid a hand on his collar. He was far too sensible to leap out of a window, but she held him firmly anyway.

"He's a nice little fella, isn't he? What is he? A terrier?"

The man leaned across, reaching out his hand. Toby

immediately forgot he was on guard duty and licked at it enthusiastically.

"Yes, he's a Jack Russell." Jayne smiled properly. Toby often gathered admirers. It was the way he looked at people with such knowing intelligence. And Jayne couldn't help but think someone who liked a Jack Russell dog couldn't be all bad, not really.

"I always wanted one of these. But the wife, she was allergic. I suppose I could get a dog now though."

"Oh, yes, I recommend it. I love having a dog. I couldn't be without my little Toby. Dogs are such good company. And your wife? Is she not allergic anymore?"

"No. She's still allergic. She's just not my wife anymore. It's easier to get rid of a husband than an allergy. Allergies stay with you for life. Husbands are disposable, apparently."

His voice had regained its surliness, or perhaps it was more of a sadness?

"Oh dear. I am sorry." Jayne sipped the wine. It was very nice, rich and oaky. A pound a glass? Two pounds, perhaps? "I take it you're divorced."

"Yes. It's been a year now."

"Oh! Snap! Although my Derek died, of course. I'm a widow."

"You're lucky. I wish my wife had died," he said morosely.

"No, that's a terrible thing to say. You shouldn't wish death on anybody. Especially after what I saw today."

"What was that then?"

Jayne settled back in her chair. It was surprisingly easy to talk to someone you couldn't actually see. "Well, I thought it was a dead body. In fact, I'm sure of it. But everyone else seems to think I'm mad."

"Oh, so that's you, is it? The crazy woman running about town shouting about bodies on the beach and such like?"

She was slightly annoyed to find out that word had travelled around already—and in such an unflattering way. "Well. I wasn't running anywhere. And I did see a body. And I'm certainly not crazy. But yes, I suppose that is probably me. Unless this happens a lot around here?"

He laughed, a short sharp snort, as if it was a sound that he wasn't very comfortable making. "No. Nothing much happens around here. Or nothing like that anyway."

"So, you're local, are you? To the village?"

"Town. It's a town. A very small one, but technically a town. And yes, born and bred here."

Jayne smiled. His insistence that it was a town not a village and his way of correcting her put her slightly in mind of Derek. Derek always wanted to get the facts straight.

"So do you reckon you really saw a body?" he asked.

"Hmm. Yes, I do." She wondered how much she should say to him. One glass of wine and a lick from a Jack Russell wasn't really a guarantee that he was a trustworthy—and he'd already wished his own wife dead.

Still, it wasn't as if he was going to reach through the window and do her a mischief. "Yes. I'm sure I saw someone, dead, you know, by the jetty, the little one over there." She gestured into the darkness, even though he couldn't see her now that he was sitting down too. "But by the time the police officer arrived, it had gone."

"Stranger things have happened," he replied, his voice sounding hollow in the darkness.

"Really? Are you sure? Because it's certainly the oddest thing that's ever happened to me." She knew she sounded a little chippy, impatient, even snappy.

He gave that laugh again, a snort this time, and puffed on his pipe. "Well, I suppose you're right. I've lived here all my life and I've never seen a dead person, let alone one who vanished shortly after."

She felt mollified. It *was* strange.

Either she was sane and of sound mind and a very odd thing had happened, or she was quite, quite mad. And surely one of the hallmarks of madness was that you weren't aware of it. So there was no point wondering if she was mad. She might as well carry on assuming she was sane and she had seen what she had seen.

Although, to be fair, her mind did seem to be rambling today, and she couldn't quite keep her thoughts straight. And, if she was honest, she would never usually be sharing a glass of wine with a strange man through a window, as if it was normal.

What would Tabitha say? She would be certain that the man had bad intentions, or that Jayne was being reckless and feckless and heckless.

Jayne giggled to herself. She was making up words now. She really was feeling a little strange.

'Settle down, Jayne,' she heard Derek saying to her. She touched the locket around her neck. Yes. Keep her thoughts to herself. That was wise.

CHAPTER 9

Jayne drank a little more of the window-wine. "So, is your wife still around?" she asked, wanting to take the focus away from her before she let on that she was hearing her dead husband talk to her more clearly than ever. She'd be run out of the village by locals bearing pitchforks. Or was that what they did for vampires?

"Yes. She's still around. Unfortunately. She chucked me out and I have to live in this dump and see her all around the place, looking happy and enjoying herself and shacking up with all sorts."

He sounded very bitter.

"I'm sorry. It must be difficult. Very difficult."

He puffed on his pipe. "And she doesn't hide it. The men. Especially that last one. Bloody Jago's the latest."

Jayne cocked her head on one side. Jay goes the latest. The grammar here was difficult to keep track of.

"Jay goes the latest?" She repeated. "I don't understand. Who's Jay?"

"Jago."

"Jay goes?" Was he making sense at all?

"Jago bloody Jenkins. Jago. That's his name." He puffed out another blast of pipe smoke, like a belligerent dragon.

"Oh." She got it now. Her brain really was slow tonight. It was all one word. "Jago? Is that his name?"

"Yes. I just said so." He spoke as if she was being

deliberately stupid.

But it fell into place. "I see. Jago. A charming name."

"Well, he isn't a very charming man. Unless you're a woman."

She'd heard someone else talking about him already today.

"Is he the boatman? On the little boats across to the Mount?" she asked.

"Yep. Part-time boatman and full-time bloody idiot. There are more kids in town who look like him than you'd credit. Why the women flock to him, I have no idea. And Caroline is just the same."

He took another large puff on his pipe and exhaled heavily.

Jayne couldn't help but cough.

"I know that cough. I heard you coughing last night. I might have spoken out of turn before." He sounded rather embarrassed.

Perhaps snapping loudly at a stranger and telling her not to get her knickers in a twist was out of character for him— although she suspected not.

He continued talking. "It's just the tourists, you know. They turn up in their thousands, clogging up the streets, wanting everything to be ice-creams and bunting and not letting a man smoke his pipe in peace."

Jayne wasn't sure what to say. Yes, he'd been very rude to her the night before, and still was being rude now. She was a tourist too, after all. "Well, I just wanted a holiday, after everything with Derek. And I couldn't help coughing. That smoke is quite potent."

"Hmm. Yes. Fair enough, fair enough."

She supposed that would have to do for an apology. And at least he was being nice enough now.

"Caroline didn't like it either. But then she goes and throws in her lot with that scumbag who smokes like a chimney anyway—and it's those cheap hand-rolled cigarettes. I can't see how that's any better."

"No, no, I'm sure it isn't," she agreed.

Really, what his ex-wife did or didn't do was no business of hers, but it was pleasant enough, drinking her wine and looking out into the night sky and hearing the gossip of the village.

The castle was illuminated at night and rose up out of the darkness as if it was hovering in mid-air.

"And it wasn't like she was the only one. I could name you the rest of his flipping harem. Mary Trelawney, for one. You'd think she would know better. The Trelawneys wouldn't be pleased about that."

"Is that the famous pasties? Trelawney's?" She remembered Mary, a little slip of a woman with a pale face and wisps of brown hair escaping her hair net who'd served her in the pasty shop that morning after all the commotion.

"Yep. The Trelawneys. Pasty royalty around here, they are."

Jayne laughed at the expression, conjuring up an image of Mary in a long red, velvet cloak, walking regally out of her shop with a pasty instead of a crown on her hair-netted head.

"You might laugh, but that shop is a goldmine. They're loaded, the Trelawneys. And if Mary is throwing it all away on that idiot boatman… Well, let's just say her brothers won't be best pleased."

Jayne considered. Could selling pasties really make so much money? There were regularly long queues outside the shop and they did seem to be an absolute staple of the diet for both locals and tourists alike. Perhaps that was Mary's brother in the shop, the one she deferred to and made Jayne hush in front of.

"And his ex-wife is still on the hook, fussing over him, making him dinners every night." Mr. Grumpy sighed and drew deeply on his pipe and Jayne recoiled slightly as a puff of smoke drifted in front of her.

"No. I don't know what that man's got, but he doesn't deserve any of it, not a damn thing."

Jayne wanted to lighten the mood. Talking about his ex-wife's lover was obviously getting Mr Grumpy deeper and deeper into the gloom. She knew what it was like, wallowing in dark thoughts. It did no good at all.

"So, tell me, what's it like here in winter? Are there still tourists?" She hoped this would change his tack onto cheerier topics.

"It's dead. It's a ghost town. All the holiday cottages sit empty, and some of the shops close down. It's bleak, very bleak."

Jayne sighed. Well, that hadn't worked at all. Apparently, summer was bad but winter was worse. She tried again. "Where do you think I should visit around here, if I want a proper walk out one day?"

"A walk? Have you got a car?"

"No. I arrived by train. My car is back at home."

"Then you've got the coast paths, in either direction. To Penzance one way. That's nice, if you want a bit of shopping. Or you could go out along by Perranuthnoe and Prussia Cove the other way. It's a good walk. I haven't done it in years."

Toby laid his paws on her knee and gave a little whine. All this mention of his favourite word was making him twitchy and expectant.

"That sounds lovely. Perhaps I'll try it. But for now, I'd better take Toby out. He's asking me rather pointedly."

Jayne was relieved to end the conversation. He wasn't an easy conversationalist, getting riled up about his ex-wife and annoyed about the tourist trade and depressed about the winters too. No wonder his wife left him.

Jayne passed her empty glass back through the window. "Thank you for the wine. It was very nice."

"Yes, yes," He seemed lost in thought again, almost as if she wasn't there.

"Well, goodnight."

CHAPTER 10

The next day, Jayne awoke feeling rather annoyed. She was still certain about what she'd seen. It was a man, a poor dead man, and no one had believed her.

What had Mr. Grumpy said? That she was already regarded as the crazy woman running about town shouting about bodies on the beach.

Hmm. Let them think that. But she knew she wasn't crazy.

Flashes of what she'd seen kept sliding into her mind.

She was making coffee, but the steady drip of the machine and the wind across the bay combined to sound like that flap, flap, flap of cloth—his coat, perhaps? And for a split-second she was there again, face to face with those cold, blank staring eyes as Toby nosed at his motionless form.

"Oh, Toby. I hope they don't find dog hairs on him and start to suspect *you*."

Toby tipped his head and looked at her quizzically.

She liked to think he was pondering the matter alongside her, but she suspected he was really waiting to see if she'd say the magic word.

She sighed and got up. It was time to go out for Toby's early walk.

"Shall we..." She'd not even got to the words 'go for a walk' before he was leaping about excitedly, his tail wagging.

She smiled down at him. He was the epitome of delight,

and all because they were going out for a stroll. His simple happiness was always infectious.

This time she tidied herself up and made sure she was presentable before going out. Perhaps if she'd looked neater and less-wild-haired, the Policeman would have taken her more seriously.

They wandered through the village—the town, she corrected herself. Perhaps it was a town. It had several churches, even more pubs and quite a lot of shops.

She stared into the window of an antiques shop, surprised to see a few things in there that she had at home. Old yes, but antique?

Toby insisted they go his favourite way, to the old jetty where she'd had her unpleasant experience. She sighed. There was no use trying to make him go a different way. If there was one defining trait of a Jack Russell it was stubbornness. For a small dog, they were utterly determined.

She followed him down the sweet little lane with its lovely cottages.

The flowers bloomed outside Kensa's door, the long white trumpet flowers looking quite elegant and striking. But next door, at Endon Cottage, the pot of marigolds had withered.

They needed watering—the irony, to be just a few steps from the entire Atlantic Ocean, and yet dying for want of water.

She checked the jetty before she clambered down onto the beach. There was nothing there.

She sighed with relief. If she'd seen something black and dark there again, huddled against the side of it, even she might have thought she was going mad.

She let Toby have a few minutes by the beach, then turned about, heading back into town. She needed hustle and bustle around her, the comfort of people and movement and distractions.

There was a nice jewellery shop, a lovely art shop with gorgeous paintings in it, and some souvenir shops too. In between was a small clothing shop, selling traditional Breton-style smocks and bags made of sailcloth.

She stopped outside, looking at the sturdy navy-blue jumper hanging up. It was a nice piece, made of thick wool, with an unusual and complex pattern across the chest.

She rubbed the hem of it between her fingers, marvelling at how thick it was. It would certainly keep the cold out.

The proprietor popped out of the shop. She was a plump woman of about Jayne's age, with a mass of light brown curls bouncing around her face as she moved around, straightening her displays, petting Toby, smiling up at Jayne.

"You're admiring the Gansey."

Jayne smiled at her, rather blankly. "It's a lovely sweater. Is it hand-made?"

The woman nodded. "Yes. It's a traditional Cornish fisherman's jumper. Me and a couple of others around here make them. But we can't keep up with demand. This is the last one we've got at the moment. We'll have some more in stock in a week or two, with any luck."

"No, no. I wasn't thinking of buying it. I was just admiring the quality. And I haven't seen a pattern like it before."

"You won't see that anywhere else. That's the Marazion pattern. Every town has its own version. But there aren't many around who can knit them anymore. It's a dying art."

"That's a shame. I love to knit. I wonder…" She traced the complex chest pattern, trying to work out how it was created.

"Ooh! You knit, do you? Are you any good?" the woman said, her evident excitement making her voice rise.

Jayne had never had her knitting habit greeted with any other than mild boredom before.

The woman continued. "You want to give it a go? I've got

the pattern. I'll buy it off you, if it's good." She was virtually hopping from foot to foot in her enthusiasm.

Jayne laughed. "Oh, I'm not looking for a job, but it is a lovely item. It would take a couple of weeks though, surely?"

The woman shrugged. "Yes. They're not quick to do. That patterning is complex. It makes them denser and warmer, especially over the chest where it's exposed to the wind. They're knitted tightly to keep the weather out. It's a skill, but like I said, I can give you a pattern. How about it? You buy the wool from me, and if the jumper's anything like half-decent, I'll give you back twice the cost of the wool. And if it's not very good, you can keep it, or unravel it and start again and use the wool for something else if you like. What do you say?"

Jayne pondered. She was knitting toys for a local charity, but she'd already done more than they asked for. She had no grandchildren to knit clothes for—and didn't modern mums prefer easy-wash clothes these days?

"Come on. If you like knitting, there's no downside for you—and you would *really* be helping me out. I'm *desperate* for more knitters. Please!"

Jayne was swayed by the women's enthusiasm and evident excitement. But she was still hesitant to get involved. "You know I'm not local—but I suppose I will be here for a few more weeks."

"Well, that settles it, then. That's plenty of time, and if you get stuck on the pattern, I'm here every day. I'm Anna, by the way. And I'll let you into a secret."

The woman lowered her voice, and Jayne stepped closer, wondering what she was going to say. Her heart pounded for a moment. Was this about the dead man? Did this woman, Anna, know what Jayne had seen? Did she know what had happened to the man?

Anna whispered, "I'm not local either. I moved here thirty-five years ago and they still call me an incomer." She laughed. "Come inside. You can bring your dog."

Jayne was disappointed the information wasn't about the man. But perhaps it was a relief too. "I'm Jayne, and this is Toby," she said, following her into the small, narrow shop.

At the far end were baskets of wool. Toby sniffed around a bit, stuffing his nose into the piles and snorting.

After a while, he decided he wasn't going to find any bones or treats or rats or anything exciting at all amongst the wool and piles of t-shirts and tea towels and stood patiently at her side.

Anna gathered up an armful of dark navy-blue balls and counted them out next to the cash desk.

"Always in dark blue. That's the only colour the fishermen wore." She took a printed pattern from under the counter and waved it at Jayne.

"Here you go. The pattern. The secret code." She paused for a moment and grinned up at Jayne, her curls falling around her face.

Jayne couldn't help laughing too. This woman's good-humour was infectious.

Anna traced down the lines of instructions on home-printed the knitting pattern. "It's not that complicated. But when you get to this part, with the cabling, just pop in and ask me if it's not clear."

Jayne studied the pattern. It looked straightforward enough, even if it was complex in parts. "And this is the Marazion pattern?"

Anna spoke with pride. "Yes. We're the only shop selling them. The only one in the entire country. In the whole world! They're unique, they really are. Back in the day, you could tell where a fisherman was from, just by looking at his gansey—his jumper."

Jayne paid a small fortune for the wool, briefly wondering

if this was some kind of hustle to sell more wool. But she wanted to give it a go, and Anna seemed like a nice woman.

Jayne thanked her, and Anna talked about the ganseys and the difficulty in getting anyone to make them anymore. "I could sell hundreds, you know, well, thirty or forty a year, but I just haven't got the knitters."

"Well, you've got one more now."

Anna was delighted and even gave Jayne a big hug before she left the shop.

Jayne smiled all the way back to her apartment. She really was starting to feel like part of the village now.

She carried the bag full of wool back to her apartment and put it on the table. She'd start that later. A new project was just what she needed.

Her holiday was improving. True, yesterday had been unpleasant in all kinds of ways. The body. The condescending policeman. The sea sickness.

It had been a peculiar day all round. She'd continued feeling odd and having rather alarming flights of fancy for the rest of the day. But a good night's sleep had seen it off and she was back to her usual self today.

She looked again at the wool and the pattern. Yes, her romantic hero would definitely wear one of these jerseys. The heroine would rest her cheek against his lovely thick jumper and feel his heart beating in his strong, broad chest.

Perhaps she would do an hour's writing and then she would have dinner and start the new knitting project and have a nice quiet evening.

CHAPTER 11

By the time she'd eaten her dinner and stared at the knitting pattern for half an hour and then at a new blank page of her writer's notebook for another twenty minutes, she was feeling twitchy.

The romance just wasn't coming and she wasn't in the mood to knit.

She tried gazing out at the lovely view, but nothing. All she saw was the cold sea, the relentless waves, the implacable tides coming and going.

"Oh dear. This won't do at all," she said brusquely. She knew these moods. Since Derek had passed, it was all too easy to get stuck in the quicksand of melancholy.

"Let's shake it off, shall we?"

Toby leapt up enthusiastically, always eager to do whatever she proposed.

"A quick mid-evening walk to chase away the blues."

He wagged his tail in approval.

She went out, this time point-blank refusing to go back to the lonely little jetty where... Well, it was best not to think about that now.

Instead, she headed in the other direction, past the big hotel-pub, and along the path behind the main beach.

The brisk evening breeze blew away her mood as she walked, and when she turned around to head back, she did feel better.

Near the pub, she passed a group of women, manhandling—if women could manhandle—a large wooden boat up the beach and into a shed.

She paused to let them by, watching them idly. What were they doing?

One of the women caught her eye and nodded.

It was Kensa, the red-head from the cottage, who'd taken her in, in her hour of need.

Jayne smiled back, glad that this time she wasn't in her almost-pyjamas, with wild hair and mascara clumps on her eyelashes.

Jayne watched as they pushed the boat into the shed, and gathered up coats and bags.

On her way out, Kensa stopped. "You're still here then, are you?"

From the women's tone, Jayne wasn't sure if it was a question or an accusation, but she nodded. After all, she could hardly deny it. "Still here," she said brightly. Perhaps most tourists only stayed a few days.

"How are you? Are you feeling alright?" Kensa asked, still staring at her intently.

Jayne smiled. Last time they'd met, she'd been on the edge of hysteria. "I'm much better, thanks. It's been just a quiet, uneventful walk tonight."

Kensa nodded. "Me and the team are going to the pub for a few, if you want to join us."

Jayne was touched by her unexpected welcoming kindness. "Oh. That's nice of you. Well, I was only really taking Toby out for a walk."

"You'll be walking past the pub. You might as well come in for one."

"Do they allow dogs?"

"Yeah. Your dog has probably got better manners than

half the people in there."

They both looked down at Toby, who was sitting neatly by her feet, doing a very good impression of a well-trained and well-behaved dog. He cocked his head, as if he agreed completely and wagged his tail.

"Well, perhaps that would be nice," Jayne said.

It had been a long time since she'd been in a pub. She and Derek... Well, of course socialising hadn't been on the agenda for the last few years, and since he'd gone, she hadn't felt much like sitting in a pub. But this big gaggle of broad-shouldered women looked friendly enough, and it would be rude to say no.

She followed them to the pub, and they headed into the downstairs bar.

It was a traditionally-styled inn, cosy, with wooden beams, old pictures, copper pots, wooden rowing oars and all manner of clutter on the walls and hanging from the ceiling.

"Pints of Rattler all round? Does that suit you, Jayne?"

"Uhm, yes," she agreed, not sure what Rattler was, but not really wanting to be the only one asking for a glass of chilled white wine.

The women sat around on bar stools or standing, talking about some upcoming races.

Jayne gradually gathered that they were a rowing team, rowing those old wooden boats, and that they were training for the championships.

She looked at them, all drinking the beer. No, not beer—it was cider, she realised as she took a mouthful. A very appley and very alcoholic cider.

This was the kind of sport she could get behind—the kind that ended up with convivial evenings drinking and everyone ordering chips and sandwiches and pasties at the bar.

"So," Kensa said, finding her way back to Jayne's side. "What do you reckon? You still think you saw something on the beach the other day?"

Jayne shrugged. She didn't want to rehash it all or dwell on it or risk further accusations of madness. She knew what she'd seen, but perhaps it was better kept to herself. "No, probably not. Like the police officer said, it must have just been someone having a nap."

Kensa smiled. "I thought so."

Jayne didn't think so, not for a minute, but she was happy to put the topic to bed. "Now, tell me more about this rowing—how long have you been doing it?"

They chatted for a while, then Kensa drifted away, eager to get to her pasty and chips.

Jayne stood by herself for a few minutes then spotted an unoccupied table. "I'll just sit down for a while," she said, to no one in particular.

It was good to take the weight off her feet and Toby leapt up onto the padded bench seat next to her and lay with his head on his paws. "Well, you've made yourself quite at home. I hope it's allowed." But Jayne could see it wasn't a fussy place.

Some of the women from the rowing team were still wet with small pools of water gathering around them. A couple had even come in with bare feet all covered in sand.

Jayne relaxed. This was a nice, peaceful place where no one bothered you or fussed about anything. It was perfect for her and Toby to have a quiet drink before she headed home.

CHAPTER 12

A familiar smell caught her attention. It was fruity, smoky and not altogether unpleasant. She looked up to see a figure she recognised.

"Oh hello! It's you," she said.

The man looked at her blankly, leaving Jayne feeling rather silly.

Then the man looked at Toby, and back at her and almost smiled.

"Oh yes. It's you, is it? The lady with the dead body."

"You make it sound as if I carry it around like a handbag."

He gave a short bark of a laugh, and Jayne noticed Kensa look over, her gaze lingering on them for a second.

"Let me buy you a drink. Another one? Rattler, is it?"

She shook her head. "I don't think I could manage another pint of this. It's rather gone to my head already. Anyway, I think I owe you a drink. What can I get you? Red wine?"

"I'll buy it," he said, and turned abruptly and went to the bar. In moments he returned, a bottle of red in his hand and two glasses.

His movements were followed by several pairs of eyes, Kensa's included.

My Grumpy sat down opposite her and poured them both a drink.

"So, have you found anything else on the beach lately?" he asked.

She wanted to sigh out loud. Honestly, you find one dead body and it sticks with you for life. Would anyone here ever talk to her about anything else?

"No, nothing of interest today. But I have been offered a commission to knit some of those lovely Cornish fisherman's jerseys, the ones they sell in that shop in the village."

"Town," he said, almost automatically. "Oh, so Anna's got you roped into her knitting circle, has she? Caroline, my ex, used to do that. Maybe she still does."

"Don't you see her very often?" Jayne gathered that they weren't in touch any more, if he wasn't sure what she was up to these days.

"I'm seeing her right now," he said.

Jayne narrowed her eyes. Was he having delusions? Did he think she, Jayne, was his ex-wife? Should she make her excuses and leave?
"Or at least, she's seeing me. I can feel her eyes burning into the back of my head."

Jayne took a hasty sip of wine. "She's here, is she?" Panic fluttered in her chest. She certainly didn't want this to be misinterpreted in any way.

Yes, she was sitting with this man, sharing a bottle of wine. She could see how it might look to someone else, but there was nothing to it, nothing at all.

"She's in the rowing team. They're all looking at us, I dare say." He smiled, clearly rather pleased to be making waves.

Jayne wasn't so pleased. She was the subject of enough gossip already, what with her rather hysterical outburst to Kensa and her mystery beach body. Being cast as Mr. Grumpy's potential love interest was certainly not something she wanted.

He was tall and quite gaunt, and perhaps he was a decent-looking man for his age. He certainly wasn't quite as surly as she'd first assumed. But she wanted to *write* romance, not become swept up in one of her own. And if she did suddenly develop urges in that direction, she was fairly certain that Mr Grumpy wouldn't be the one to rekindle that long-dormant flame.

"And is *he* here—her beau?" Jayne was rather curious to see this Jago, the wife stealer, the heartbreaker, the Lothario.

Mr Grumpy gave a quick glance around. "No. You'd know if he was. He'd be holding court. He's loud. Loud and full of it. Always laughing and joking about something." The tone he spoke in was as if he was describing some kind of bizarre and despicable behaviour.

"But he's not around at the moment. I hear he's gone AWOL again," he continued, sounding slightly more cheerful

"He does that often, does he?"

"Yes. he's probably chasing another woman somewhere. Caroline won't be pleased," he said with glee. "Nope. Not very pleased at all."

"But isn't he a ferryman? Don't his employers mind if he just disappears?" Jayne was thinking about the other boat people's complaints, on that morning when she had been so ill.

"He's got them over a barrel—he owns the slipway and the other jetty—the high tide one. A couple of times a month, the boat from the Mount has to dock there. But it can't do that if the old sod doesn't give them permission. So, if he doesn't turn up to work for a couple of days? What are they going to do? Sack him? I wish they bloody would. The place would be better off without him."

Mention of the jetty had sent her mind back to that morning and the sight of the man's face, dead and cold. She shivered at the recollection and pulled her mind back to the present—the lively pub, the clink of glasses, the loud chat, the smell of old pipe smoke emanating from Mr. Grumpy mingling with the whiff of hot pasties and frying chips.

"What does he look like, this Jago?" she asked, a thought

curling like a wisp of smoke through the back of her mind.

"Like an ordinary bloke," he replied, rather unhelpfully.

"Short, tall? Fair-haired? Dark?"

"Dark, I suppose. But nothing special. I don't know why women go for him."

So much for the garrulous locals. She needed details. 'An ordinary bloke' didn't narrow it down much—except maybe it did...

What *had* her dead man looked like? How tall was he, for example? The trouble was she hadn't much been in a measuring mood... She'd been in more of a screaming and running away kind of mood if she was honest.

But he was dark haired, and nothing unusual about him stood out, not to Mr. Grumpy anyway. So it hadn't ruled him out. But if it *was* him, why wasn't anyone looking for him?

The answer came quicker than she'd expected. "Anyway, he'll have gone up country again and be shacked up with some new woman. Probably someone he chatted up on the boats."

"Up country?"

"Out of county. He's left Cornwall, chasing skirt, as usual. So, there'll be a few tears around, and some burnt pasties," he added with satisfaction.

"Really? Why? Burnt pasties?" Was that just a local phrase to show that people might be out of sorts or distracted, or did he actually mean it literally?

"I told you. Trelawney's?"

"Oh, yes," Jayne nodded, remembering him gossiping about the pasty woman also being in thrall to this Jago man.

A few burned pasties wouldn't bother her. She wasn't about to revisit the pasty experience any time soon. The last one had been the victim of her sudden seasickness and the associations weren't good.

Mr. Grumpy refilled their glasses. "They never learn,

these women. He's bad news, all round. Maybe he won't come back this time, and good riddance to him."

He raised his glass as if in a toast, and took a drink, then turned and looked pointedly over his shoulder.

A blonde woman in rowing gear glared back at him. She was tall and slim with a smooth blonde bob, looking far too elegant to be Mr. Grumpy's ex-wife.

"I think Toby needs a walk," Jayne said, not happy about becoming an unwilling and unwitting corner in his love triangle.

"I'll walk back with you," he said, quickly downing the rest of his glass and picking up the bottle.

This was even worse. She didn't want to be seen leaving with him, but there was really very little option.

She could, perhaps, escape to the ladies' lavatory, like they did in sitcoms, and wriggle out of the toilet window, but knowing her luck, it would be directly over the sea and she'd end up in the sea, and then everyone would definitely think she was insane.

She gave in to the inevitable and walked out of the pub with her new man friend.

She called a good night to Kensa and got a rather odd grinning salutation in reply. The blonde woman was too busy glaring at her ex-husband to look at Jayne.

She overheard a rather loud comment as she passed, something about, "Some fancy piece from up London."

Startled, she realised it might be directed at her.

Well, I'm neither fancy nor from London, she thought. But she couldn't deny that it was quite a novelty to be cast in the role of 'other woman,' however mistakenly.

She smiled at the thought. A temptress in a raincoat and sensible shoes. Well, it takes all sorts.

A short walk later and she was back at the apartment

block.

Mr. Grumpy hadn't spoken all the way, and Jayne suspected his only interest in her was in arousing the jealousy of his ex, which was rather a relief.

They entered the building together and said a brief good night, and let themselves into their adjacent doors.

She sat for a few moments with her notebook, wondering about a love triangle for her romance.

Perhaps her heroine could be a wronged woman, cast aside. Was she taken in by a dastardly rake, who swept her off her feet and then abandoned her? The true hero could come to her rescue and fight a duel with the rake.

The hero would win of course, but be injured and she could nurse him back to health. But she knew from nursing Derek that there was nothing particularly romantic about it. Maybe a love triangle wasn't going to work.

She closed her notebook and made sure Toby had his food and water for the night.

As she got ready for bed, a rather unpleasant thought struck her.

If the dead man *was* Jago—and she had a strange sinking feeling that it might be—then her next door neighbour could well be a prime suspect.

If Jago was the reason that his wife, Caroline, had left Mr Grumpy, then of course he'd hold a grudge.

Was Mr. Grumpy an actual murderer?

CHAPTER 13

The next day, she was determined to make the journey across to the Mount. Her entry tickets were still valid and she wasn't going to take the boat. No way. Not this time.

Toby didn't mind at all. He was as perky as ever, delighted to be going out. "It's the only way to avoid the boats," Jayne explained to him. "If we walk over later this morning, the tide will come in while we're there and we'll have to get the boat back. I can't face that."

Memories of her ill-fated boat ride were still too strong to risk it again. No. This was much better. She had her tickets, and she could visit in peace and be back again before most of the day-trippers had even arrived for the day.

It was shockingly early and she knew that the regular tourists, on the whole, didn't come out until ten am. Until then the town was quiet, populated by locals 'getting on with things' before the stream of visitors choked the streets, causing queues and traffic chaos.

This morning, she'd even beaten the locals and the town had been deserted as she'd walked though its silent streets.

Dawn had barely broken and she was already waiting on the beach for the tide to fall low enough to reveal the broad stone pathway on the sea-bed, snaking across the sand, toward the island.

After a few more minutes of waiting, she decided it was time. The tide was ebbing away and each time a little more of the pathway through the sea was revealed.

Walking across the still-wet path, lapped on either side by the water as the sun rose was quite magical. It was like being in a fairy tale.

At the lowest part, she had to wait a while longer for the tide to keep falling so the last part of the path would be out of the water. Toby loved every minute of it, splashing through the inch-deep water and snuffling at piles of wet seaweed.

Then she was at the island. She walked through an elegant stone gateway and she was in another world. Little terraced cottages hugged the edge of the harbour. There were a couple of shops, and cafes, but some of the cottages looked like actual homes.

One or two other tourists were here too, early risers as well and they shared a complicit smile, knowing they had the best of the day to themselves.

Imagine living here, Jayne thought. You would have to check the tide times to get on and off the island, and be completely cut off for half the day, every day, except for the tourist boats. Did the boats even run in winter? What a peculiar lifestyle it would be.

Perhaps her heroine could live here, stranded like Rapunzel in the tower, but with rather less hair.

Behind the granite cottages, a rather grand entrance-way led up to the castle gardens.

Semi-tropical plants abounded, with palm trees, succulents, and even the tall spires of echiums growing happily.

Her hero and heroine would walk through these gardens, hand in hand. *'My love for you is as tall and strong as this palm tree,' the salty fisherman whispered.*

Jayne stopped for a moment on a bench and sat down, scribbling her ideas into her writer's notebook, before she forgot them.

'And mine glows as brightly as this carpet of flowers,' the

heroine responded, gazing adoringly into his bright blue eyes.

Eyes. Were his eyes brown or blue? She couldn't remember, even though it was important. It was all about the eyes in romance. Blue eyes. Brown eyes. Violet eyes. Cold, dead eyes.

She shook the thought away. That was the day before yesterday. She wasn't going to let those memories intrude today.

She looked more closely at the lovely little star-shaped flowers her heroine was referring to. She must find out what they were called.

She leaned in, trying to read the label that was attached. Delosperma. It sounded rather suggestive. Could her heroine really say *'And mine glows as brightly as this carpet of delosperma,'* Or was the plural delospermums?

Jayne frowned, rather annoyed that the flowers didn't have a more poetic name.

Perhaps she'd change it. Forget-me-nots? Now that was a much nicer name for a flower. Some things couldn't be forgotten. *'I'll never forget you, my love,' her heroine murmured.*

But then a vision of the dead man floated into her consciousness again. She would never forget seeing that. Or the way his face looked, so cold and grey.

"No. No dead men today, thank you," she said tartly, and stood up, trying to dispel the vision from her mind.

A passing tourist looked at her with slight alarm, and tightened his grip on his wife's hand and quickened his pace.

Jayne smiled wryly. Perhaps talking aloud to Toby wasn't a good idea.

She continued up the steep path, exploring the delightful gardens.

Everywhere were rocky outcrops, plants seeming to balance at impossible angles, occasional patches of vivid colour, and all surrounded by the sound of the sea and that bright clear blueness it gave to the light.

Toby was on his best behaviour, enjoying his trip out. Two walks was usually his allowance, so when Jayne went on a big expedition like this, he loved it.

When the cafe opened, she was one of the first in there.

She sat at an outside table, sipping her tea and eating a freshly baked scone with jam and cream. It was a real treat, especially at this time of day, but she felt she'd earned it.

Getting up early wasn't easy, but she felt very pleased at how much she'd already accomplished.

Toby had a drink from the doggy bowl outside the cafe. A nice touch, to welcome our four-legged friends too, Jayne thought, approvingly.

She wondered if her heroine might work in the cafe over here on the island. It was rather a nice image. Jayne noted it down in her Writer's Notebook. The page was filling up nicely with scraps of scenes and various ideas.

Once she'd finished her tea, she felt ready to go back to the mainland.

She might do a few hours of proper writing this afternoon and try to turn some of these ideas into an actual story.

"Time to go home, Toby?" she asked. He wagged his tail. But he did that whenever she spoke to him, so it wasn't much help really.

Still, it was nice to have the company, even if her canine companion wasn't much of a conversationalist.

She left the Mount, walking the stone pathway slowly, looking at the rock pools and the shining wet sand on either side. There were a lot of people coming the other way.

They're just beginning their day out, she thought, rather smugly, while she had been up for hours already and was on her way home.

The walk across was the nicest part, she decided. It would be a delightful setting for part of her story. Perhaps the hero and heroine could be stranded on the island as the tide swept in, or stuck halfway back to the mainland, and the hero had to pick up the heroine and carry her as the water rose around his feet. That would be a nice scene.

If he was strong enough. Jayne calculated the distance back to the shore. It was quite a long walk.

"*I'll carry you, my love,*" she murmured, trying out the words.

Toby looked up at her quizzically.

"Not you, silly," she said.

But the stones were slippery. What if her hero fell over? Or what if he carried her for a while and then his arms ached and he had to put her down again?

Of course, as was usual in these stories, her heroine would be slender and small, not a sturdy burly girl with broad shoulders who ate pasties and scones every day. And her hero would be tall, dark and handsome, naturally, and easily able to carry his love-interest. But it was still a long way.

Jayne pondered. Perhaps the tide would only start coming in when they were close to the shore, she decided.

Reality shouldn't impinge too much. It was romance, after all, a lovely escape from reality, but all the same, it was a long way to carry someone.

Her mind wandered. People were heavy, even slender young women.

So who could have carried off the dead man she'd seen? He was a biggish fellow, from what she remembered. And if he hadn't been carried away, what *had* happened to him?

Jayne sighed loudly. That poor fellow would keep coming back into her mind, just when she was trying to picture a romantic scene with her hero rescuing the heroine.

Like an unwelcome intruder, the face of the dead man kept swimming into her consciousness.

"Come on, let's pick up the pace," she said brightly to Toby. He was happy enough to oblige, trotting along next to her, his tail raised like a wagging flag of happiness.

Soon enough, they were back at the beach.

The whole broad sweep of sand to the left was speckled with tourists, with wind-breaks, umbrellas and brightly coloured towels spread out as far as she could see.

To the right, where the beach was narrow and rocky and strewn with seaweed, there was no one.

She could see the jetty over that way—the one where the dead man had been.

Of course, the tide had come right in and out again several times since she'd seen it.

Any evidence would be long gone.

Would she ever get to the bottom of the mystery of the disappearing dead man? Or would it remain an inexplicable almost impossible event, to resurface and trouble her on sleepless nights for years to come?

Perhaps he *had* been sleeping, she tried to tell herself. Perhaps she had imagined the whole thing. Stress. Grief. It could do that to someone.

But she knew in her heart that she hadn't imagined any of it. He had been there.

She stepped off the path, and decided to head over to the right, and make her way up to the set of steps over there. It was a more direct route back to her apartment, and it would save her from going through the town.

She would get home, have a hot cup of tea and make a few more notes in her writer's notebook. She had some nice scenes in her mind now and they would soon start coming together into a story.

She left the path, making her way between the rough rocks, skirting around the deeper pools, and climbing across the low-lying rocks, some slippery with seaweed.

Toby was enjoying it immensely. There was no one around this side, so she let him off the leash and he ran around, snuffling the sand and chasing shadows.

Then she saw it. A flapping of black cloth against the base of the rocks.

She shook her head. "No more visions, today, thank you," she said under her breath. She'd had quite enough of those the other day.

But the noise continued, a flap, flap, flap of material caught by the wind.

Toby approached, growling low in his throat as if he didn't like it.

Jayne wanted to just walk away. To ignore it. Not to look. But she couldn't.

She took a few steps closer and saw a hand, a man's hand, outstretched, damp, covered in sand.

No. No. *No.*

It couldn't be.

Not again.

She was breathing fast, her heart pounding.

Toby pushed his nose under the pale-blue hand and it flopped lifelessly back onto the sand.

CHAPTER 14

She watched Constable Jefferies wander down the beach.

When he saw her, he stopped dead. "Oh no, not you again," he said, really rather rudely. "What is it this time? Another false alarm? Another man having a nap? Wasting Police time, that's what this is. You can't keep doing this."

The helpful tourists that she'd asked to keep watch looked askance at her then, as if they'd been taking instructions from a madwoman.

But Jayne ignored his rudeness and led Officer Jefferies around the rock.

With a triumphant flourish, she pointed at the thing she didn't want to look at. "Voila! There you are! One dead body!"

Jefferies stared at the sight and then went green. His face fell in shocked disbelief, then something like panic, before he threw up on the sand.

He staggered off to vomit again behind a rock.

Jayne would normally have felt sorry for him, but she had almost no sympathy at all. In fact, she couldn't stop smiling. "I told him. I told him two days ago there was a body," she said to the rather bemused German couple standing guard with her.

They took a few steps back then, as if her evident glee was inappropriate and even alarming.

She tried to keep her smiles to herself since then, but my goodness that had been a very satisfying moment.

"Voila!" she repeated softly to herself, recalling her grand arm gesture as she revealed the body.

Jefferies' face was a picture. His patronising smile had been wiped clean away, replaced by shock and alarm.

Oh, yes, it was almost worth not being believed the first time, just to see his face this time.

Once he'd finished being ill, Jefferies had called for more officers to attend the scene.

The poor Germans had given their names and left, no doubt with a rather less positive view of Marazion and a strange story to tell when they got back home.

Jayne stood there almost proudly, guarding the body as Jefferies ran back up the beach to get a signal and made some calls.

Soon, several more uniformed officers arrived, along with a Detective Chief Inspector.

A very grand title for quite an ordinary looking man, Jayne thought, as he introduced himself to her as DCI Pollard.

He had stood next to the deceased for a while, looking at the scene without speaking and then ambled slowly over to her, as if this whole thing was just a run of the mill event.

He leaned down to pet Toby, then straightened up. His grey eyes swept over her, and Jayne was very glad that this time she wasn't half-dressed and all in a muddle.

This time was different. This time, they would have to believe her.

Finally, he spoke. "So, you're Jayne Jewell. Jayne with a y. The person who called in with the non-existent body the other day. Not satisfied with that, you've come back for a second attempt. And this time, you have actually got a body for us. You're getting better at this." He nodded, as if he was impressed by her tenacity. "Well done, Jayne with a y. A significant improvement."

Was he making a joke about this?

Jayne had to contradict him. If her first interaction with Jefferies had taught her anything, it was to be more sure of herself and to trust in what she'd seen. 'Don't let this official write you off too, Jayne,' she heard Derek's voice saying to her .

Despite his seniority, his grand title and his air of gentle mockery, she had to tell the Inspector that he was wrong. "Actually, I did have a body the first time too, but no one believed me."

"Hmm. Perhaps you did."

Well, that was an admission of sorts, she thought. At least he was entertaining the possibility that she'd seen a body before. It was better than Jefferies' flat-out disbelief.

"But," he continued, "Is it the same one? What's more unlikely—an uninvolved stranger finding two different bodies, or someone finding the same body twice?" DCI Pollard looked at her as if he was trying to solve an amusing little riddle rather than dealing with a scene of death.

He cocked his head slightly to the side and for a second, he reminded Jayne of Toby.

Her dog did exactly the same thing when he was trying to work out Jayne's intentions too. Except Toby was only ever wondering if she was going to share her food with him or take him for a walk.

She rather suspected the Inspector might have darker concerns.

Why had he almost seemed to give air quotes to the phrase 'uninvolved stranger'? She *was* uninvolved, and this was just an unpleasant coincidence.

Jayne had been trying not to look at the rock behind which the poor man lay, colder and bluer than even before, but she knew what she'd seen. She knew it was the same person.

"It's the same man. Yes. I've found him twice. And no one is more surprised than I." She felt a slim surge of pride at ending her sentence with the more correct form of 'I' rather than 'me.' She wouldn't have this policeman looking down on her like Jefferies had done.

She suppressed a smile at the memory of how she'd put Jefferies firmly in his place by actually finding a body again. 'Voila,' she murmured to herself.

"Are you enjoying this?" The Inspector asked. There was a tone of mild amusement in his voice.

Jayne stopped smiling, realising that it could be misinterpreted as callousness or even something worse.

"No. Not at all," she hastened to assure the Inspector. "I feel terribly for the poor man, I really do. But—But..." Should she say anything else? She looked up at the Inspector. Somehow, she trusted that he would understand.

She carried on. "It's Jefferies. He didn't believe me, the first time. He was rather condescending, actually. So, this time, well, he had to believe me..."

They both looked over at Jefferies. The young policeman was leaning on a rock, hanging his head, still in the midst of illness.

"You're not suggesting that you deliberately found a body in order to prove Jefferies wrong, are you?"

"Of course not. It's not as if bodies are like sea shells, littering the beach. You can't just *decide* to find one," she said, a little more acerbically than she'd intended. "No. I just wanted him to know that I had seen it, that first time," she explained.

Jayne thought she saw a smile flicker across the Inspector's face too, just for a microsecond.

"Hmm. I read Jefferies' notes about you on the way here. Apparently, you were 'verging on the hysterical' and 'not making sense' and 'rambling about cold dead eyes,' according to his notes." The Inspector tipped his head and looked at her intently, as if trying to weigh up whether or not she was likely to suffer from hysteria.

Jayne was outraged. "I was *not* hysterical. Not at all." Maybe she'd come across as a bit flustered. She'd been all alone and in shock.

"Well, I was shocked of course." she explained. "Panic had set in. I couldn't get a signal on my mobile. It was early in the morning. I hadn't even had any coffee," she explained, trying to get across the series of events that had left her all upset, trying to run across a beach, asking strangers for help, quite alone and out of her depth with it all.

"Aah, yes, a dead body is far better once one's had some coffee," the Inspector said.

She frowned at him, not sure if he was being sarcastic or not. "Yes, well, I may have seemed rather perturbed. But not hysterical. I'm not used to seeing dead bodies, you know. Surely a little hysteria is a reasonable reaction. I'm not a sociopath."

"Well, you're calm enough now," he offered. "Perhaps you're getting used to it. In fact, I believe you gathered witnesses to guard the body, and sent someone off to call the police. Very calm. Very sensible."

She hoped the Inspector wasn't suggesting that she was too calm, too organised this time. "Well, I didn't want him getting away a second time."

"Dead bodies can be a little frisky," he agreed.

She wanted to laugh, but that didn't seem appropriate. They were only ten feet away from where the poor man lay.

"Well, I better get on. Time and tide wait for no man, especially a dead one. But, Jayne, with a y, I'll be in touch. I want to get to the bottom of this—a drowned man is no surprise around here, unfortunately. But they don't usually disappear and reappear of their own volition. You're sure, are you, that he was well out of the water, the first time? There were no waves lapping at his toes?"

She shook her head. "I'm sure. He was about as far from the water's edge as we are now from him."

He nodded thoughtfully. "Thank you. I have all your details, thanks to Jefferies, and I'll be in touch soon."

CHAPTER 15

Later, Jayne called her daughter. The call did not go particularly well.

"Not two dead bodies, darling. The same one twice, on different days." Out of habit, she held the phone to her ear, even though Tabitha's face was on the screen.

"No. I didn't keep going back to it. I found it and lost it and found it again."

She paused as Tabitha exclaimed in horror and then seemed to almost blame Jayne for the strange events on the beach.

"Yes, yes, I know Tabitha. It does sound rather odd."

Jayne allowed Tabitha to talk for a little longer, agreeing with her. It was quicker that way.

"Yes. I'm sure Mr. and Mrs. Ainsley didn't have anything like this when they had a holiday in Cornwall. I don't think most people do, darling."

She looked at the phone screen, as Tabitha went on, and on. Her face was the spitting image of Derek's. It was more feminine of course and softened by her long hair, but all the same, it was like having a young female version of Derek berate her.

Jayne sighed loudly. Why was Tabitha acting as if Jayne had deliberately set out to find bodies?

"Don't sigh like that, Mother. Now, did you call the Police?"

"Yes, yes, of course I did." Did Tabby think that Jayne would stumble across some dead bodies and just walk merrily on her way, leaving them there, without a second thought? "The police came both times. Officer Jefferies was the first one, a young man with acne. He wasn't very good. But then today there were more of them, including a rather more senior chap. He was a DCI. An Inspector Pollard."

Jayne wondered briefly if he should take over as the model for her romantic hero—a tall, weather-beaten man who had the look of someone who'd spent long hours outside, perhaps tracking down ne'er do wells and dangerous types. He looked big enough to be handy in a fight, and yet had a rather wry manner that amused Jayne.

In her novel she might shrink his rather dominating nose, tidy up his hair and trim his eyebrows, and generally handsome him up a little. Not that he was unattractive, but men in their fifties often became a little unkempt if left to themselves, and he was no exception.

But a police officer wasn't the same as a sea captain or a fisherman. There was probably a lot of paperwork and not much time for romantic liaisons.

She dragged her mind back to her conversation with Tabitha. "Yes," she repeated to Tabitha. "The Senior Investigating Officer was actually quite impressed with how I handled the crime scene." Jayne was enjoying using this new vocabulary. Crime scene. Senior Investigating Officer. It made her feel rather important.

She added, "In fact, the Inspector even suggested I consider joining the police force."

She didn't tell Tabitha that DCI Pollard had suggested that she join as a sniffer dog, due to her uncanny ability to sniff out dead bodies.

Tabitha was outraged at this too.

Jayne hastened to reassure her. "No, darling. I'm not

actually going to join the police. That's absolutely enough crime to last me a lifetime already. I can't imagine wanting to seek it out."

Further accusations followed.

"No. No. I don't have a crush on the Inspector either. No, darling, now, it's rather unfair to say I'm chasing dead men or living ones. And one does not lead to the other anyway."

Tabitha was still talking as if Jayne was living a life of danger and wantonness, chasing murders and men with equal enthusiasm.

She calmed her daughter. "I really don't think there's a killer on the loose. It was just one man and he probably simply drowned, you know. People do that sometimes. It's just an unfortunate accident."

"No," she had to agree, "They don't tend to do that in Hertfordshire, what with there not being much sea around. Yes, it probably is safer there, but no, I'm not coming home just yet.

Look, Tabby, dear. I absolutely *promise* to be careful, and not get involved in any more crime or such like."

Finally her daughter seemed mollified.

"I'll call you tomorrow, darling. Yes, I'm perfectly safe. Yes, yes, the door is locked. Bye."

Phew.

She ended the call with a sigh of relief.

She knew she needed to tell Tabitha.

A reporter had been asking questions earlier and it seemed that this death might even make the newspapers. It was better Tabitha knew about it now, even if she had fussed endlessly, and seemed to suggest Jayne was somehow magicking up the dead on purpose.

Jayne settled back in her chair, and smiled.

The DCI had been very much more on top of events. He had seemed to believe everything she said too. And when she'd finished, he'd said, "If you think of anything else—any odd details, anything you've noticed, tell me. You have my number. It strikes me that you are a woman for details, and you may see things others overlook."

She smiled her agreement, wondering if 'an eye for detail' was just the police code for being a bit nosy. But she hadn't gone looking for any of this. She just wanted a nice, quiet, peaceful holiday in a pretty village by the sea where she could relax and knit and write her book.

All of this was just an annoyance—an upset—interfering with her plans. But, all the same, she had walked back home with a spring in her step. She had the Inspector's number. He thought her unusually observant. She might have important details. Yes, it was nice to be needed.

Jayne settled in her chair, picking up her knitting, wondering if she could get going on the gansey for Anna or if she was more in the mood for writing.

She was really starting to feel part of the community now —discovering bodies wasn't exactly the way she would like to become a part of local life, but it was certainly effective.

As if to prove her point, there was a loud rapping on the door of her apartment.

CHAPTER 16

Toby leapt up, barking and running at the door, determined to protect her from whomever it was.

At home, it was usually the post-lady. Toby took great delight in barking her away each morning, and even sometimes bit and pulled at the letters as they came through the letterbox. It was quite usual for all her correspondence to arrive slightly chewed at the corners.

She should get one of those post-boxes like the American's had, perched at the end of her driveway—but then Toby would miss the daily excitement of protecting her from the deadly incoming paper missiles.

She opened the door, wondering if it was the police again. Or Anna from the shop. Or perhaps that Inspector was back already with ore questions.

But it was Mr. Grumpy. He was with another man— blonde good-looking man in his forties or thereabouts, who stuck his hand out and introduced himself.

"I hope we're not disturbing you. I'm Daniel David Penhaligon, Property Developments, Sales and Marketing, based in Truro of course but we have offices here too."

It all came out in such a smooth rush that she could barely get a grip on what he was actually saying.

His hand was outstretched and automatically, she shook it.

"I was wondering if I could just cast my eye over the place?" he said, already moving in through her doorway.

She looked at Mr. Grumpy, bemused.

"He's thinking of buying them—the whole block. He just wants a quick look in, with yours having the best view and all."

Jayne stood back and let them in, her hand on Toby's collar.

Of course, Toby didn't bite, and he was more likely to give someone a few exploratory sniffs and then either bark at them relentlessly, or decide they were the best of friends and follow them around happily.

As a guard dog, his main deterrent was his persistent barking. No one could stand it for long. Even the most determined burglar would give up and try somewhere else if they had Toby barking in their ear constantly. But he was quiet enough now.

Nevertheless, she kept him close as the two men came inside.

For a second, she wondered if this was wise. She'd had her suspicions about Mr. Grumpy already and now she was letting him in and another man too.

She picked her phone back up. "I'm just in the middle of a call to my daughter. She likes to know who I'm with and what's going on." Jayne spoke into the phone, hoping neither of the men would notice that the screen was blank. "Yes, darling. It's the neighbour and another man. A property salesman. They've come in to look over the place." She smiled at them, but neither of the men were taking any notice of her, or her attempts to make them understand she'd identified them and left a clue, a trail, in case anything happened to her.

The one with the long name stood at her window looking out over the bay. "This is an exceptional view. He's sitting on a gold mine here."

"Not that he deserves it," Mr Grumpy muttered.

"But this all needs to go. It needs ripping out and starting again. I mean, look at it!" The blonde man gestured to the kitchen-dining area, as if it was some kind of abomination, rather than just a little tired and dated.

Aren't we all, Jayne thought to herself, feeling rather saddened by the thought of her homely apartment being torn apart.

The blonde man poked his head into her bathroom and bedroom, shaking his head. "There's a lot of work in it to bring it up to scratch, if we're going to get high-end visitors paying top whack."

Jayne would have tidied up if she'd known someone was going to come nosing around the place, but he wasn't interested in how she was looking after it. Views, fixtures, fittings, decor—they were all that was on his mind.

"But I can definitely do something here. If I get the whole block and bring it up to scratch."

The man turned to her, his smile like a searchlight fixing on her face.

He handed her a card, and addressed her with a practised charm. "Any property requirements in the South-west, I'm your man. Small, large, new home, second home, holiday home—you name it. I can satisfy all your property needs. Just give me a call." He held her gaze for a second too long. "Promise? You will call me, if there's anything at all I can do for you?" he said.

For a second Jayne was entranced by him and she felt a little flutter in her chest as he held her gaze and made her promise to call him.

With his nice blue eyes, the unlined tanned face, those straight almost too-white teeth, and his charming manner, he really was very easy on the eye, but then he was gone.

Jayne dropped his card into the fruit bowl on the table.

Salesman's tactics, she thought, dismissively. That's all it is. His card could sit with her single apple and rather green banana, and the ferry tickets—her own and the one she'd picked

CLARA PENROSE

up on the beach that time.

"Thanks, Jayne. See you later," Mr Grumpy said, following the tall man out, closing the door behind him.

"Well, it doesn't look like we'll be staying here again." Jayne said to Toby. "By next year, I imagine this place will have been redeveloped and only suit the 'high end' tourists. I don't think that's us, is it, Tobes? So we might as well make the most of it while we're here. But let's have a cup of tea and get back to that writing first."

Toby seemed to agree, and settled down again.

She jotted down a few ideas. Now her hero was tall and blonde and tanned. A handsome blonde fisherman with surprisingly good teeth. He could rescue her easily, scooping her up in his arms as she weighed nothing. Or would she rescue him?

After her success earlier that morning, securing the crime scene and putting Jefferies in his place, Jayne felt perhaps her heroine wouldn't wait around to be rescued after all. She might in fact do some of the rescuing, or at least find the hole in his boat and stop him from sinking at sea.

Sinking. Drowning. Oh no. The dead man was back, living in the recesses of her mind. Would she ever be able to write this romance, or should she just give up now?

At least when she thought of death and passing, this new drowned man had taken over from Derek, she thought, wondering if this was much of an improvement.

Jayne knew that the general consensus among her friends and acquaintances was that she was supposed to be getting on with things and rebuilding her life and making new memories, now Derek had been mourned sufficiently, but she wasn't sure that getting mixed up in a sudden death was what anyone had had in mind. But it was effective.

It was certainly keeping her busy and taking her mind off the loss of her dear husband. And he was still here too, speaking to her when she needed him.

"Oh, Derek, what would you have made of all this nonsense?" she wondered, putting down her pen and turning on the television instead.

CHAPTER 17

By the next morning, Jayne woke up with a nagging feeling that she knew something important.

That body on the beach—when Toby had nosed at the hand, it had been pale and white with a tinge of blue. And yet the tip of the forefinger and thumb were stained yellow. Smoking. The man was a smoker, and no doubt of those hand-rolled cigarettes favoured by some.

Was it enough of a reason to assume she knew the identity of the dead man?

Would DCI Pollard think her an utter fool if she called him with her suspicions? But he'd said he needed to talk to her again, and to let him know if she remembered anything else.

Well, this wasn't exactly a memory—more putting two and two together...

'Am I just leaping to conclusions?' she asked Toby, as she made her morning coffee and put two slices of bread in the toaster.

But Toby had no opinions on the matter, and was giving her that, 'Just hurry up' look.

She poured her coffee and waited for her toast.

She'd learned already not to go out in her scruffy clothes or without making herself look respectable. You never knew what was going to happen.

Toby could wait for ten minutes, while she washed her face and got dressed, and ate her toast and jam, and finished one cup of coffee.

Then they'd take a walk, and after that... Well, perhaps she should call the Inspector and share her idea. After all, it couldn't do any harm. Then it was up to him if he followed it up or not.

Her mind made up, she drank her coffee under the beady and impatient eye of Toby. He gave an exploratory yap.

She tried to hush him, but he barked again.

Getting the message, she poured the rest of her coffee into her travel cup and left the apartment, one slice of toast still in her hand.

Heading straight down to the beach—the one with the fisherman's jetty, she sat on the wall sipping her coffee and pondering.

Could that have been Jago, lying on the beach—twice? Or was he really off 'up country' with another woman? And if it was him, had he just fallen out of his boat one night, washed up, washed away and washed up again?

Jayne watched the sea, lapping peacefully at the shore, listening to the rhythmic sound of the waves. It was so lovely, so calming—and yet fatal, perhaps. A few too many Rattlers, an ill-advised boat trip, and poor Jago was a goner.

But he hadn't stayed gone.

Toby was done with his morning business, and she'd finished her coffee.

Heading back up the lane, she saw a familiar figure, standing outside her hero's cottage, giving it the once over.

"Good morning," she said brightly, doubly-pleased she'd taken the time to make herself look presentable this morning.

But the handsome blonde man looked blankly at her, as if he hadn't met her yesterday or looked around her apartment.

He nodded politely and gave her a smile. But she knew he hadn't recognized her. Trying not to feel slightly peeved, she went back to her apartment.

His entrancing gaze of yesterday, the way he'd held her eye and made her 'promise' really was all part of his salesman's trade. He hadn't got the slightest idea who she was and no memory of even meeting her. She hadn't registered with him at all.

Jayne knew she was being silly to be annoyed, but for a second yesterday she'd really thought that this handsome, polished gent was rather spellbound by her—and who wouldn't be flattered by that?

Back at her apartment, it was time for a second coffee, and to decide what to do. She checked the time. It was still not quite eight am. Did Police Detectives work a nine to five schedule?

By a quarter past eight, she decided to call him anyway. She could tell him her idea, and then forget about it for the day. Perhaps she'd take a walk along the coast, along to Perranuthnoe and beyond.

She called the number on the Inspector's card, wondering if she'd get through to one of those irritating voice mail boxes.

But he answered in person after three rings.

"DCI Pollard," he said.

"Ah, hello. Good morning. Yes. It's Jayne here, Jayne Jewell, from yesterday, from the beach, I am the one who—"

He interrupted her. "Jayne Jewell. Yes, Jayne with a y. I know exactly who you are."

At least *he* remembered meeting her, she thought, still smarting slightly from the way the other man had completely blanked her. Although of course the DCI wouldn't be a very good police officer if he forgot the names of all the witnesses and suspects he encountered.

"Well, I just called because I had an idea about who the man was—the one on the beach."

"Oh yes. And what was this idea?" He sounded faintly amused, which wasn't the response she expected.

"I think it might be a man called Jago Jenkins."

He paused, and Jayne wondered if she'd overstepped the mark somehow.

"And why do you think that, Jayne Jewell?"

She rather liked the way he used her full name—but was it rather threatening? Was she in trouble? "Oh no reason, not really," she replied.

"Hmm. Let me get this straight. You called me at eight fifteen in the morning to tell me it might be Jago Jenkins, but you've got no reason to think that. Jayne... Tell me."

She felt silly now, putting it into words. Her certainty had vanished and her suspicions seemed thin and weak. "Well, he's gone missing, or at least he's not around. And he was a smoker. He smoked those little hand-rolled cigarettes. And the body that I saw—it had yellowed fingertips. So, I just thought, maybe it was him. Maybe it would help to tell you."

"Hmm." The Inspector seemed deep in thought. "I think we'd better have a meeting, you and I."

"Oh really? I'm not in trouble, am I?" she asked, his serious tone making her nervous. She'd expected him to thank her for her tip-off and that would be the end of it. Perhaps she'd hoped for a compliment about being insightful or observant, but nothing more—certainly not this feeling of being under the spotlight of his scrutiny.

"Are you at home today?" he asked.

"I was going to walk along the coast path towards Perranuthnoe and on from there to somewhere called Prussia Cove. But I can do that another day."

"No, no. Continue with your plans. What time are you leaving?"

"In about half an hour."

Right. Then I will meet you at ten am at the beach cafe in Perranuthnoe. It's called Dolphins. You can't miss it. You'll be ready for a break by the time you get there, and then you can continue with your walk."

"Oh, yes, that's…" But he'd already ended the phone call.

She stared down at her mobile. Why did he want to meet her? Surely she wasn't a suspect? If she was, she'd be going into the police station, not meeting at a beach cafe—unless he wanted to catch her off her guard.

"Oh Toby. This is turning into a very peculiar holiday," she said, as she got ready to go.

CHAPTER 18

Jayne set off along the coast path, heading out of Marazion.

The path ran along the edge of the rocky granite cliffs occasionally dipping onto a remote beach and then back up on to the cliffs. With the sea sparkling on her right, and the rise of the wild scrubby land on her left, it was quite beautiful.

Golden gorse flowers bloomed, scenting the air with faint whiffs of coconut, and at her feet there were small hummocky clumps of bright green foliage, topped by masses of pink flowers, held aloft like little balls on stalks, waving in the breeze.

Some of the clumps clung at angles in rocky crevices and even seem to hang off the cliff face, a hundred feet up, dangling over the precipice, but still gaily waving their pink pom-poms as if they didn't have a care in the world.

To his annoyance, she kept Toby on his leash—the path was too close to the edge of the cliff to let him run loose. He pulled on it, always wanting to be three steps ahead of where he was, but she wasn't giving in or letting him go. One sniff of a seagull and he'd be chasing it, without a thought to the cliff edge and the long drop below him.

The sea was a deep blue, crashing against the black rocks, deep and almost foreboding. She tried not to think what it would be like to slip and fall. She had to banish gloomy thoughts. They weren't suitable for a beautiful day like today.

Every now and again, she took a breather, turning back to look at Mount's Bay and the lovely island — which looked even better from this angle, with its tall castle atop its rocky peak.

As she walked, she felt more at peace.

Even the prospect of an interview with the Police Inspector couldn't dampen her mood.

This was what she'd come for—the beauty of the scenery, being out in nature, the sea spray in her hair, and Toby loving every minute of it.

Her mind turned to her writing. She really needed to get on with it. That was her main reason— or rationale—for taking such a long holiday by the sea. She had planned to write for hours every day—to tell the story of her hero and heroine, to conjure up romance and passion and even heartbreak.

But so far all she had was a few pages of notes, half-formed ideas, with a few scribbled descriptions of her hero, who kept changing from day to day, and who just wouldn't come into focus.

Perhaps her tall, fair-haired charmer was more villain material, fooling around with the heroine, drawing her in with his good-looks and sweet-talking, before casting her aside, and moving on to his next conquest. Yes, perhaps that would be it.

Her red-headed heroine might be a fallen woman, secretly adored by the handsome down-to-earth fisherman.

Perhaps he had loved her for years, watching in dismay as her head had been turned and her heart broken by the handsome lothario. The sturdy, reliable fisherman would put the pieces of her broken heart back together again.

She rather liked that phrase about putting the pieces back together again. She said it aloud, trying to commit it to memory. It was far too windy up here to get out her notebook and pen.

In the distance, she could see a cove, and a crescent moon of golden sand. This must be Perranuthnoe.

The path dropped down into the little inlet, and she was glad of the shelter offered by the headlands that enclosed it.

There was a wooden hut, near the top of the landing slip, and a few tables scattered in the field next to it.

Was this the cafe?

Jayne tried to smooth her hair, but the salty spray had made it wild and disobedient, and it felt like straw.

'I wonder how my heroine will stay pretty,' she wondered, knowing the wind had made her cheeks and nose glow red and her hair a mess. 'She'll have to be a little weather-beaten, if she ever leaves her cottage.'

She looked around, but there was no sign of the Inspector.

Checking the sign above the wooden hut with its serving hatch, she could see it was indeed Dolphins cafe.

She ordered a cup of coffee, and then thought, blow it, and asked for a slice of the lovely -looking chocolate cake that sat under a glass dome, its layers rising temptingly, the cream just oozing out a little.

Toby had a noisy drink from the bowl placed outside.

She paid for her coffee and cake and chose a bench table in the garden, sheltered by a tree.

Sitting down, she took out her notebook. Now what was the phrase she'd liked? *'Mending the broken pieces of her heart, one by one.'* That was it. She scribbled down a few more ideas, and some descriptions of the sea and the coastal walk.

Her pen poised, she wondered how to describe the sea, jotting down her thoughts. *'Sparkling. Blue. Wavey.'* Surely she could do better than that? 'Wet.' No this was getting worse.

She chewed the end of her pen before remembering how expensive it had been. Come on, she chided herself. A nice description of the sea. She could come up with something better than blue and wet and wavy.

CHAPTER 19

"Jayne Jewell."

The voice startled her and she jerked her head upright. She'd been quite lost in her own world, and almost forgotten she was expecting company.

She patted her chest. "Sorry. You made me jump."

"Creeping up on people is all part of my stock in trade," the Inspector said amicably.

He nodded to her dog, greeting him almost formally. "Hello again, Toby."

Then he turned his attention back to Jayne. "Another coffee? More cake?" he asked.

She shook her head. If she had two pieces of that chocolatey delight, she might never shift from the bench again. "I'm fine, thank you."

"Right. I'll just get myself something and be right back."

Jayne closed her notebook and petted Toby's head, and then scooped a few little bits of the cream from the cake onto her finger and held them out for Toby. It wasn't terribly hygienic, but Toby didn't seem to mind and licked it enthusiastically. He looked at her plate as if trying to hint that there was more he could have. "Dogs shouldn't have chocolate," she told him. "I'm sorry, Toby, but it's bad for you."

DCI Pollard returned and sat across from her, not quite opposite.

"Are you making notes? Finding more clues?" he asked,

looking at her notebook.

"Oh, no. Not clues. Just a few ideas. I'm trying to write a novel. It's not going terribly well so far."

"A murder mystery, is it?" he asked.

She laughed. "No. It's a romance." She was surprised she'd said it so readily.

She hadn't told anyone else what she was up to, but somehow, the Inspector invited confidences. There was something slightly comforting about his rather unkempt eyebrows and those grey intelligent eyes.

But perhaps it was his training. Maybe his whole demeanour was designed to get people to confess their darkest secrets—although writing a romance—or trying to, at least—wasn't exactly a crime.

"A romance. Good for you."

She was rather pleased he hadn't scoffed, or looked surprised or laughed at her.

"So you're a writer, are you?" he asked.

She nodded. A writer. Well, perhaps she was. She'd been a wife, a mother, a carer and then a widow. It felt good to be something else, something new.

"I thought you might be something like that. You strike me as the artistic type, but observant. too."

It was nice to hear she actually looked like a writer. Perhaps her rather wild hair gave her a devil-may-care poetic look, although she suspected that observant was the police code-word for nosey.

"I haven't written much yet. Things haven't been terribly conducive to peaceful romance writing, since I arrived."

"No, I imagine they haven't."

He took a sip of his coffee. It was a rather extravagant-looking cappuccino. He wiped the fluff from his top lip.

Jayne sat there, not sure if she should make small talk, or

if this was a police interview, of sorts. You didn't go about asking the police officer about his day or if he liked the scenery.

DCI Pollard got down to business. "You said on the phone that you thought the deceased might be one Jago Jenkins." He looked at her again, his eyes kind but unwavering, as if he wouldn't stop looking until he found the truth.

"It's probably nothing, but I thought I might as well tell you. It's just that he's disappeared, you see. Rumour has it that he's off with a woman somewhere. But I just thought it was an odd coincidence. And then there was the smoking too—and those stains on the fingers of the poor man on the beach. It just seemed to fit."

The Inspector nodded, but didn't say whether he agreed with her or not—or if he knew the identity of the body.

Jayne remembered what else she'd wanted to tell him. Was it worth mentioning?

"There's something else too. It only came to me earlier. I don't know why I'd forgotten all about it. It just didn't seem important at the time. It probably isn't. No, I'm sure it's nothing."

He seemed to find her slightly amusing. "Tell me. I'll decide if it's something or nothing."

"Well, the night before the first time I saw the body...." She paused, wondering if he'd challenge her on the fact that she'd seen it twice, and dispute that there ever had been a 'first time.'

But he didn't interrupt, except to say, "So this would be the night of the fourteenth."

"Yes, well, I was down at the jetty, the same one where, in the morning I saw him."

"You seem to spend a lot of time at that jetty, hanging around there. Does it have a particular appeal for you?"

She frowned at him, not liking the insinuation that she

PASTIES, SAFFRON BUNS AND MURDER

had some kind of ulterior motive for 'hanging around' at a jetty. "I don't care for the place one way or the other," she said, with a little asperity in her voice. "But Toby is a creature of habit. Mostly bad ones, I'm afraid." She reached down and fondled the dog's ears. "And he led me down there, the first night and now he likes to visit the same spot every day—for his business."

"Aah. I see. You can't come between a dog and their business. Continue." he seemed to suppress a smile.

"So, I heard some voices. They were talking about the tides and whatnot, and about just doing something. 'Once he's in, he's in.' I'm sure that's what one of them said."

"Did you see them? How many were there?"

"Two, I think. I didn't see their faces at all. I just heard them, walking along the beach, talking about tides and if it was the right time to do something, and about doing it, tonight."

""Well, it is coincidental, perhaps, with the location being the same. But you don't know who they were. You didn't actually hear anything incriminating. And trying to hang a case on some unknown people talking about the tides next to the fishing jetty probably isn't a good idea—not if I want to stay being an Inspector."

"But it's a piece of the puzzle, surely? When you think about it—they could have been plotting something."

"Hmm. The problem with having pieces of the puzzle that are open to interpretation, is bending them to fit the space we have."

"If it's a puzzle, you'd be jamming them in, not bending them," she said, thinking of doing a jigsaw.

"Well, yes. Indeed. But the fact is the same. Useful titbits, Jayne Jewell. All useful. But in and of themselves... Just supposition."

"I suppose it is." Then she laughed. "Excuse the pun." Did that count as a pun? To suppose it was supposition?

He must have thought so too, because he smiled at her, shaking his head slightly.

He had a nice smile—warm and friendly, and somehow, with his grizzled, rather scruffy hair and his unkempt eyebrows, he rather reminded her of Toby. He was probably just as stubborn and insistent on following a trail as Toby was.

Jayne sighed. She'd thought she'd had a good clue but the Inspector didn't think so. A 'titbit' wasn't exactly a crucial piece of evidence. He probably secretly thought she was as deluded as that first policeman, Officer Jefferies, had done.

CHAPTER 20

But the next thing the Inspector said made her feel a lot better.

He said, "However, if it wasn't for your initial sighting of a body—or your claim to have seen it—we would in all likelihood be writing this off as a drowning. Unfortunately, it's not uncommon. Despite spending a life on the sea, many of the fishermen can't actually swim and most of them don't wear life jackets. If one falls in at night, or when they're alone, it would be hard for even an accomplished swimmer to survive. However, your statement that you'd seen the body two days earlier, in a different location, puts a slightly more interesting slant on things."

She sat up a little. Her information about the men in the night-time might not have struck a chord, but she was still central to this case.

"Now, I have Jefferies account here. Let's have a look at it." The DCI pulled out a notebook and flipped over some pages. "The witness was seen earlier going down to the beach, talking to herself, in a dishevelled condition. Ten minutes later, she returned, hysterical and incoherent, claiming to have seen a dead man on the beach. She was talking about trumpets and heaven and cold, dead eyes. On investigating the scene, I found no evidence of a body. I concluded the witness was suffering from confusion or a temporarily disturbed mind." He closed the book. "That's what Jefferies said."

"Well! For a start, I wasn't dishevelled, thank you very

much. It happened to be very early in the morning and Toby insisted on going out and I just hadn't bothered to brush my hair or get properly dressed. And for another thing, I wasn't talking to myself. I was talking to Toby." She knew she was getting a little aerated.

The DCI grinned at her. "Talking to Toby, hm? I imagine he speaks more sense than a lot of people."

"Hmm. Well, he's a good listener, and if I don't speak to someone, the silence can drive me mad sometimes." She remembered how hard it was when Derek stopped talking, and she had hour upon hour of silence.

The radio and television helped, but it was talking to Toby that kept her sane—even if talking to him was now regarded as a mark of insanity.

Was it considered a little crazy to talk to a dog? No. Not unless you heard him talking back. Now that might be cause for concern, although she was sure Toby would only say wise, sensible things, mostly related to walks and smells and food and being allowed to sit on the sofa and have his ears petted.

"He doesn't talk back to me, you know. I just say things out loud to him, to break the silence," she explained. "He likes it. He likes being talked to, don't you, Tobes?"

Toby jumped up, wagged his tail and pushed his wet nose into her hand.

The Inspector smiled at the dog. "So, you hadn't got dressed properly and you were simply talking to your dog. That sounds reasonable enough. Let's accept, for now, that you aren't a raving lunatic."

"Thank you," she said, not entirely sure that was the nicest thing anyone had ever said to her. But something else was bothering her. How did Jefferies know she'd been talking to herself on the way down to the beach?

"Kensa must have told him, before he got to the house. Jefferies didn't ask me about the way down to the beach. But

I'd seen her, first, before I got there." Jayne felt rather betrayed. Kensa had told the police that she'd seen Jayne acting like a lunatic. No wonder Jefferies didn't take her seriously from the outset.

"Kensa. This would be one Kensa Jenkins, of Primrose Cottage, Opie Lane."

"Yes. But… She's called *Jenkins*?" Jayne stared at him. "Like Jago Jenkins?"

The DCI inclined his head.

"But that's odd, isn't it? Both called Jenkins?" Jayne felt like someone kept throwing more pieces of a puzzle into her jigsaw. Just when she thought she was getting the hang of it, something else was thrown into the mix and the picture changed all over again.

The Inspector looked unexcited by her point. "Many of the towns and villages around here are dominated by a handful of families. Marazion, for instance, has the Jenkins, the Joses, the Penhaligons, the Pengellys, the Trewarthas and a few incoming Trelawneys, although they're mainly based in Penzance, of course."

Jayne was still looking at him, her head on one side. "Where did Jago Jenkins live?"

"You know. You were ranting and raving outside his cottage, according to Jefferies' notes."

"*His* cottage?"

"Endon Cottage. Next door to where Miss—no, it's Mrs, I believe, Jenkins lives."

"Hmm. That's odd. That lovely little cottage."

There was silence for a moment, then she slapped the table. "The marigolds died," she exclaimed, "Because he couldn't water them. Because he was dead."

"Hold on, Miss Marple. You're frightening the children."

Jayne looked around to see a toddler staring at her from

the next table.

She lowered her voice. "The flowers outside his cottage. I was admiring them the first morning, but now they've died. They're all dried up and dead. Kensa took hers away too, I wonder why. They were lovely white flowers, Angel's Trumpets, I believe. Not primroses at all. They should have been primroses."

She dabbed her lips with a paper napkin. Life seemed so fragile sometimes, so easily snuffed out, and yet others —those delightful pink flowers clinging to the rocks—seemed determined to live, against all the odds.

"Angel's trumpets. Like the trumpet call to heaven?"

He was reading from that annoying little notebook again.

"Well, perhaps I was rather beside myself. It was early in the morning, and it really was a horrible shock. Perhaps the name of the flowers had stuck in my mind, and then when I saw him... It still gives me nightmares, you know."

The Inspector nodded thoughtfully. "I'm sure it does. Artistic, sensitive too. It's hard to get over, the first time." He paused

Jayne was just thinking how sympathetic he was when he said, "I assume that was the first time that you've seen a body?"

Jayne gave him a rather annoyed look. "Well in these kinds of circumstances, yes. There was my husband, of course. But that was different."

The Inspector looked at her sharply. "Your husband. Has he passed away? Recently?"

Jayne nodded, a lump forming in her throat.

"How did he die, if you don't mind me asking?"

CHAPTER 21

Jayne stared at him, the realisation sinking in.

Goodness. The Inspector suspected her. Inspector suspected. The words tumbled together in her mind.

Was she really a suspect in the case? Did he think she'd bumped off her husband and then come on holiday and done away with some other poor soul—that she was some kind of serial killer? A black widow, killing off any man who came too close?

No. That wasn't fair. Not at all.

She frowned at him, suppressing the tears that threatened. "My husband died of a very long and unpleasant illness. He passed away last year," she said.

She wasn't going to get into the details.

DCI Pollard's face softened. "I'm sorry to hear that. It must have been difficult."

She nodded again. "It made it worse. Seeing the man on the beach. It reminded me. Not that Derek—my husband—drowned. Or was anywhere near a beach. Or looked anything like him. Or happened like that, out of the blue," she added, just for clarity.

She certainly didn't want the Inspector to think she had some propensity for drowned men. She emphasised the point. "Before I came here, I certainly hadn't come across any other dead men on my walks with Toby. And I hope I never will again."

DCI Pollard smiled. "That's good to hear. I'm sorry. I had

to ask. It's an ingrained habit now, I'm afraid."

Jayne wasn't exactly mollified. She didn't expect to be treated as a suspicious character.

He fixed her with that kindly gaze again. "Tell me more about that morning. Tell me everything you remember about when you saw the body, and then what happened after that. Everything."

This, she could do. Jayne took a sip of her coffee and launched into it, in as much detail as she could.

It was nice to be listened to. Finding that body on the beach, the first morning, had been a terrible shock, and she'd had no one to talk to about it—or at least no one who wasn't looking at her with patronising disbelief. It was therapeutic to get it all out, and to someone who listened with such rapt attention.

He checked occasional details. "When you went back and the body had gone, the sand was disturbed, you say. Describe how, exactly."

"There were footsteps, lots of them, in no clear trail, and longer marks, like drag marks."

"Going up or down the beach?"

"How can I tell?"

"Were the marks above where the body had been, as if it had been pulled off the beach up onto the coast path or the jetty, or below the body, toward the sea?"

She thought hard. "Between the body and sea. As if it had been pulled down to the water."

"And how far out was the sea?"

"Not far—maybe about ten feet from where the body had been."

The Inspector looked something up on his phone. "High tide was about six am. You think you were there about seven am. It's possible that the tide could have washed the body in and deposited it there. But it couldn't have taken it out again, not within that time frame. For that, we have the footsteps, the drag marks and so on." He consulted the notebook again. "Jefferies didn't make a note of them."

"Well, I'm afraid Toby got rather excited and scattered a lot of sand. He could smell something."

"Disturbing a crime scene, hm?" The inspector looked down at Toby, who wagged his tail as if he was proud of himself.

There was another thing though. Jayne said, "And the ferry ticket I found? Do you think that's a clue? I've still got it, you know."

"Jefferies didn't bag it up and take it away?"

She shook her head. "He wasn't interested. He said there are thousands in the town. Or Kensa said that. I suppose they're right."

"All the same, he should have logged it." The Inspector looked stern and rather fierce for a second, and Jayne wondered if Jefferies was going to get a talking to. Rather him than me, she thought.

"Wet or dry?"

"Excuse me?" Jayne looked at him, not sure what he was referring to.

"The ferry ticket. When you found it."

"Oh. Dry."

"So, it wasn't from the man's pocket."

Jayne had missed that detail. Anything that had come from the man was bound to be soaked through. But at least the DCI seemed to fully accept she had indeed seen a body and that it was all rather suspicious.

"So, who moved the body, Jayne?" He held her in his gaze.

He didn't suspect her, surely?

"Well, it certainly wasn't me, Inspector!"

"No, no, I didn't think it was. But who was it? I think if we solve that mystery, we'll be on our way to getting to the bottom of it."

"So you think there *was* foul play?" She leaned closer and hushed her tone. "Was it a murder?"

He sat back and smiled at her. "We can't jump to conclusions. I'll gather evidence, I take statements and I see where it leads. Preconceptions can be misleading."

Jayne was rather disappointed. She had hoped he would confirm that it was a murder, that the victim was Jago Jenkins, and that she, Jayne, had helped enormously with the investigation. And maybe that she could help him to solve the rest of it. But he didn't.

"Anything else? What did you do, after your interview with our best police sleuth, young Jefferies?"

Jayne smiled at him. "Well, nothing much. I bought a pasty. I was going to go over to the Mount that day but when I got in the boat, I felt ill, so I didn't. I spent the rest of the day in bed."

"Ill?"

"Sea sick, I think, although I've never suffered with that before. But maybe it was because of the shock. I've never come across a dead man before either."

"No. I suppose not." He regarded her for a few more minutes, as if he had more questions, but he didn't ask anything else.

"Are you continuing your walk along the coast to Prussia Cove?"

He was changing the subject. Was the meeting over?

"Yes, I think so. It's been a lovely walk so far, really beautiful."

The Inspector looked around. "Yes. I've not walked this stretch for a few years now. I should do it again sometime."

Jayne had a crazy idea to invite him to join her. He would be good company. But he was a policeman, and at work, and why on earth would he want to?

"Well, I can certainly recommend it," she said, lamely. "Toby will enjoy it."

"He certainly will."

The Inspector stood up. "Thank you, Jayne. I may need you to come down to the station and make a formal statement, if this looks like it will become a criminal investigation. You'll be in the area? At your current address?"

"Oh yes. I'll be there for another three weeks. It takes more than a dead body to scare me off!"

She waved at him as she set off, Toby on his leash, back down towards the coastal path.

There was spring in her step, and she was smiling to herself as she walked. Why was she feeling so cheery, all of a sudden?

"It's a beautiful day, Toby, and a lovely walk, and perhaps I just feel better for getting it all off my chest."

Toby seemed to agree, giving her a wag of his tail, and then continuing to sniff along the ground, as if he was following secret trails of his own.

"Yes, that's it. That's all it is," she told herself, as the path started to climb up the rocky headland.

CHAPTER 22

The next morning, when she popped into the local shop for some milk and a sliced loaf, Jayne saw the newspaper headline, and a picture of an all-too-familiar face.

'Marazion Man Dead, Presumed Drowned,' read the headline, then in smaller letters underneath, 'The body of Jago Jenkins (46) was found on Marazion beach. Police are treating the case as accidental death.'

Jayne stared at the article. The man's face seemed to follow her everywhere. But in this picture, he was alive— laughing, happy.

"This is such a sad business," said the lady at the till, seeing Jayne staring at the headline. "I knew him. We all did. It's shocking."

"How terrible, losing a man like that." Jayne couldn't resist digging, just a little bit. "His poor wife and his family, they must be distraught."

"Well, I don't know about that. His wife was his ex, more or less, and that was a difficult relationship. And as for his kids— well, let's just say not many of them know he's their father." The woman gave a grin, as if her grief was a very thin layer atop a deep desire to gossip about the dead man.

"Really? How so?" Jayne asked. This was more like it—a lovely garrulous local, prepared to spill the tea.

She was a middle-aged woman with a tanned face and dark, close-cropped hair.

With glasses on a chain around her neck and her smart

white blouse, she looked more like a very efficient library manager than the gossipy proprietor of the local grocery shop.

"He was a gadabout. Half the kids in the village have his dimples, but their fathers are none the wiser. And Kensa, well, she had enough of it, but even she couldn't leave him alone."

"Kensa was married to Jago?" Jayne asked. "But they lived next door to each other." It seemed a very odd arrangement for ex-partners.

The woman at the till didn't seem surprised that Jayne knew who they were and where they lived. Perhaps that was just normal in a small place like this.

"Of course she was. She didn't want to let him go either. He let her have that cottage out of the goodness of his heart, and she used it to stay close to him. Maybe he liked her seeing all his women coming and going. He was quite a fellow. He was always up to something. Women, wine and... not song. More women, usually." The woman laughed.

She clearly wasn't too upset by his death. "I'm going to sell out of these today," she said happily, patting the pile of newspapers on the countertop. "A tragedy always shifts extra copies."

"Gosh, yes. I'm sure it does. Everyone will want to read about it. And you say he had a whole lot of children out of wedlock?" Jayne wanted to squeeze a little more information out of the woman. This was the first person she'd met who seemed eager to talk, even to a complete stranger like Jayne.

Then the bell on the door jangled. "Morning, Katie. Lovely day. Pipe tobacco, my usual."

Jayne turned and smiled at the man. It was Mr Grumpy, looking much more cheerful than she'd ever seen before.

"Oh hello, Jayne. Nice day, isn't it? You're out early. Morning, feller." He gave Toby a pat on the head and turned back to the counter. "I better take one of these scandal sheets too," he said, picking up a newspaper. "So, old Jago's gone. That'll leave more than a few beds cold at night." He grinned at his own comment, not even pretending to look sad.

Jayne was annoyed that her rather fruitful conversation was at an end, but seeing Mr Grumpy being not so grumpy at all was making her think.

"Jayne," the woman at the counter said. "Oh. I thought you looked familiar. You're in here too. You found him, didn't you?"

Jayne nodded. Her picture was in the newspaper? Where on earth had they found a picture of her?

She hung around in the rather cramped shop, looking at a carousel display of postcards and wondering if many people bought them anymore.

Perhaps she should send one to Tabitha. She chose a nice one of Mount's Bay, and returned to the counter.

"The funeral's already arranged for next week. They must want him in the ground quickly," said the chatty shop proprietor, Katie.

"I'll be going to it, just to make sure the bastard's buried down deep," Mr. Grumpy said, with relish.

"Oh, by the way, the shop will be closed on Tuesday, for the funeral, you know. We'll all want to go. I'd better make a sign to put up," Katie said.

"Do you think Trelawney's will be closed?" Mr. Grumpy said to Katie. They shared a complicit look and laughed.

"Not likely," said Katie. "Not while there's money to be made."

"And they won't want to pay any kind of respects to that man," Mr. Grumpy added cheerfully.

"Can anyone attend the funeral? I'd like to pay my respects." While that was true, Jayne also wanted to see who was there and what was going on.

The woman at the till, Katie, smiled at her. "It's an open

funeral. Anyone can go. And I'm sure you'd be welcome anyway, as you're the one who found him," she said.

"There will be a fair few women there. You'll blend in with the crowd," Mr. Grumpy added.

Katie lowered her voice, clearly relishing the chance to gossip. "A lot of women knew Jago very well indeed."

"There will be some sad, lonely women around now," Mr. Grumpy declared, looking positively delighted at the prospect.

"Oh no, not me. Not like that! I only saw him after… You know, once he'd…" She didn't want to put it into words, but she definitely didn't want Katie or the rest of the town to think she'd been one of his harem.

"Don't worry. Your secret's safe with me," Katie said, smiling again.

Jayne didn't have a secret, and she was almost completely sure that if she had, it wouldn't be safe with this woman, but there was not much she could do about it now. Katie seemed determined to hang onto the idea that Jayne had been more to Jago than the mere discoverer of his body.

Other people were coming in and Katie had turned away to talk to them.

Jayne paid for a newspaper, her bread and milk and the postcard and a stamp too, and took her purchases home. At least there she would be safe from insinuations that she was part of Jago's extensive harem of women.

CHAPTER 23

Sitting at her table, Jayne spread out the newspaper and looked at the picture of the dead man. He wasn't dead in the picture, of course. It looked like a photo that had been taken in a pub, probably the same one she'd been to. It showed him laughing and shiny-faced and full of life.

He was a handsome man, she decided. With his thick dark hair and his charming smile and the dimples that gave him a rather appealing, even devil-may-care look, she could certainly see his appeal.

He looked a little rough around the edges, as if he might smell of the sea and wet dog, but he'd be ardent and passionate and amusing, and before you knew it, he'd have charmed his way into your bed.

Not mine, of course, Jayne hastened to assure herself, despite what Katie and Kensa had assumed.

Why had so many women fallen for him? She gazed at his picture, trying to imagine him full of life. He'd convince you that you were the only woman with a place in his heart and his bed, and then he'd be gone by morning.

Jayne opened the window to let a little cool air in. This was all rather heated for so early in the day.

Perhaps Jago would make a good role model for her romantic hero—he might have a dangerous, salacious past, but when he settled down with his true love, he would become a faithful, loyal husband. Tamed and utterly devoted.

That hadn't happened with Jago though, she mused.

Apparently, he'd been married to Kensa. And he had still lived next door to her, or rather she lived in the cottage he'd given her.

He was a generous man, then, and happier than most to keep his ex-wife close.

She scanned through the other photos of him in the article inside the newspaper. They had given it a lot of space —the story dominated the front page, and then a further two pages inside, but there wasn't much other news to compete with the story.

The other pictures of Jago showed him as a younger man, standing by the ferry boat, another of him in a smart suit, at his wedding perhaps?

She read it all carefully. There was no mention of his ex-wife or any children, but it did mention his father, a Petroc Jenkins who had been a miner until the local mines closed. He'd gone overseas for a few years, working in foreign mines.

Jayne was rather shocked to turn the page again and see a picture of her own face looking back at her. It wasn't a terribly good picture. It had been taken from a distance, showing her standing on the beach, next to the rocks. Behind those rocks lay poor Jago Jenkin's body. But it was definitely her. Her green and yellow jacket was unmistakable and Toby was by her side too.

Who had been taking pictures. Was it one of those tourists who had helped her stand guard? Had they snapped a picture of her and given it to the newspaper?

Her name was printed underneath too with the line, 'Holidaymaker Jayne Jewell discovered the body.'

Tabitha wouldn't be at all pleased if she found out Jayne had made it into the local newspaper on her supposedly quiet and safe holiday.

Jayne flicked through the newspaper looking for any other information.

The other stories of the week were an article about parking charges increasing, and a second one about a Royal

Mail post-box that was out of use because too many snails were getting inside it and chewing up the letters and making them slimy. Not exactly big news.

She paused when she came to four pages crammed with advertisements for houses for sale. A quick scan of them shocked her.

She wondered how Jago had afforded to own two cottages, his own and Kensa's next door.

These quaint little seaside cottages were worth an absolute fortune, if similar properties were anything to go by. From being fishermen's huts, they had risen to become very desirable sea-view homes, perfect for a holiday home or for renting out to so called 'high-end' tourists.

She tapped a pen against her teeth. That was a lot of money—an awful lot of money. And who would get it? Who would inherit the cottages? And what about poor Kensa? Did she own her cottage?

Katie had said, 'he let her have it,' but did that mean he'd given it to her or simply let her live there? If they were still married, surely she half-owned it anyway, or would do now Jago had passed on?

Jayne mused on, wondering where this train of thought would take her. 'Follow the money,' she heard Derek's voice saying in her mind. That was always his mantra when he was doing his tax fraud investigations. 'There's nothing in this world people won't do for money. It's the most powerful force in the world,' he'd told her.

She'd disagreed with him at the time. 'Surely love is stronger, Derek. Jealousy, passion and so on.'

But he'd argued against it, saying that money was how people showed their love and passion, how they controlled others, how they took revenge.

Jayne wasn't convinced. In the romantic world she was constructing—painfully slowly—love would be pure and untainted by money or greed. But all the same, Derek's insistence that it all came down to money in the end made her think.

Jago had been sitting on a fortune, and perhaps that had led, somehow, to his untimely death.

And yet the police were treating it as accidental.

She sighed irritably. She had thought better of that Detective Chief Inspector. He seemed an intelligent man who would always get to the bottom of things and yet Jago Jenkins death was being written off as accidental. How could it be accidental if his body and upped and moved that morning. It couldn't have done that by itself. There was nothing accidental about that.

Jayne pushed the newspaper aside. This was all getting in the way of her writing. Every time she tried to conjure up a lovely, passionate story about two people simply falling in love, she was assailed by Derek's voice telling her money was more powerful, or by a memory of Jago's face—alive or dead —convinced he could be the Casanova of the parish with no retribution.

Was *that* why he'd died? A love rival, a scorned woman, a man who was sick of Jago's philandering ways… Even perhaps a man who had seen his own marriage destroyed by Jago Jenkins?

What about Mr. Not-Very-Grumpy-Anymore? Surely he couldn't have committed such a terrible act, just because his wife had left him and taken up with Jago? And yet, if her own views were right, then love and jealousy and vengeance were the strongest forces out there. Could even a rather uninteresting, pipe-smoking cardigan-wearing man like Mr. Grumpy could become a heated, passion-filled killer?

"Oh, I just can't see it, Toby," she said. A jealous lover should have a little more swagger, a little more charisma than Mr Grumpy.

And yet, love could drive the mildest of men to do the

most desperate of things.

I'd better not tell Tabitha I'm living next door to my number one suspect, Jayne thought. I'll never hear the end of it.

On that note, she took out her postcard and decided to write it. "Having a lovely time." Well, that was partly true. It was certainly taking her mind off Derek and all of that. And since she'd been here, she hadn't felt at a loose end, or wondered what the point of getting out of bed was—not once. So, while it might not be everyone's idea of a nice holiday, she felt more alive than she had done for a long time.

"The weather is good, and the people are..." She paused for a moment. 'Murderous' might be putting it too strongly.

There was, if her suppositions were correct, certainly one murderer among these mostly pleasant townsfolk, and perhaps he was even living right next door to her.

She imagined herself trying to explain it to Tabitha. 'But, darling, he's very particular about his victims. He only murdered the man who was having an affair with his wife, so I'm perfectly safe.' She wasn't entirely sure that Tabitha would be content with her explanation.

As to the rest, well, they ranged from friendly, like Anna in the Knitwear shop, and Katie in the grocery shop, to 'not as nice as she'd hoped,' like Kensa.

Hmm.

Her pen hovered over the postcard. 'Interesting.' That would do and at least it was true. The people were interesting.

'Toby is enjoying his walks by the beach, as am I,' she continued, before signing off, 'With much love, Mum.' That would do.

It was nothing Tabitha didn't know already, but it was just nice to send a card. And later, she'd settle down to some writing and some knitting and get to grips with the gansey.

CHAPTER 24

Jayne had a relaxing few days with her writing and knitting. It was just what she needed.

This was what it was supposed to have been like, she thought, enjoying the peace of the town and the fresh sea air.

No bodies. No disturbances. Just peace and quiet and getting on with my writing.

But her quiet time couldn't last. Today was the funeral and Jayne was going to attend it.

It had been almost a week since the news article was printed, but no one had come knocking at her door wanting interviews or anything. Apparently, her notoriety was limited and short-lived.

She was rather disappointed, if she was honest with herself. When she'd stumbled over that body, she had something to say and people wanted to hear it.

"Well, it's an ill wind that blows nobody any good," she thought to herself. It was terribly bad luck for poor Jago, but it had certainly given her a something new to think about.

"I shouldn't be thinking like that. Honestly, I'm turning into a ghoul, getting involved in things like that and feeling all self-satisfied because of it," Jayne chided herself.

Once the funeral was over, she would put the whole business behind her and forget about it all. There would be another week and a half of real relaxation, and then back home to her normal life.

Except... Except... She was still puzzled by the body disappearing that first time. There had to be an explanation. But the Police had ruled it a drowning and so there it was. Nothing out of the ordinary. Nothing to worry about.

But she knew what she'd seen, that first morning. And she couldn't quite let it go.

Jayne was about to leave the apartment for a brief stroll before she had to get ready for the funeral.

She heard movement in the corridor outside her door.

Was it Mr. Grumpy going out? She had been consciously avoiding her neighbour since she began to suspect that he might be a murderer. She kept her window closed at night, and rushed off if she saw him in the street.

It seemed rude, but she wasn't sure exactly what the etiquette was in these circumstances.

Could she avoid him for the rest of her stay? It was difficult as she was living next door to the man.

Presumably, as long as she, Jayne, wasn't having an affair with his wife, she would be perfectly safe with him. He wasn't an indiscriminate killer.

She hesitated at the door, looking down at Toby. "But all the same, perhaps it would be better to just hang on here for a few minutes until he's gone," she said, softly, her nerves getting the better of her.

But she couldn't wait too long. The funeral was later today and Toby wouldn't get a good walk this afternoon.

She looked down at Toby. He was wagging his tail already. He'd watched her put on her shoes and her coat and he knew the signs. She was going out and he wanted to come too.

"Well, if you think it's safe enough, I suppose it can't hurt," she said to him. Maybe she would pop into the shop if it was still open this morning and see if the chatty woman, Katie, was there and pick up a few more titbits. Then she could share them with the Inspector. He was bound to be at the funeral too, wasn't he?

The heavy downstairs door banged closed. Whoever it was had left the building.

"Come on. The coast is clear. We are definitely going out," she said to Toby.

She walked down to the beach first, to the thin rocky strip where the day-trippers didn't go. Despite what she'd seen there, that first early morning, it was still Toby's preferred route, and it was ideal for him. Much better than the crowded beach on the other side.

Here, he could go off leash and have a good run and she didn't have to worry about him scattering sand over sunbathing tourists or sniffing hopefully at their picnic lunches.

She rounded a rock and stopped in her tracks, horror rising up like bile.

She closed her eyes for a split-second and opened them again, the blood pounding in her ears. No. No. It couldn't be!

It couldn't be happening again!

Was she going mad? Was she seeing things? No!

It was him! And he was moving.

He clambered to his feet in front of her.

"It's you!" he said, his eyes fixed on hers.

The dead man reared up at her, walking towards her. His arms were stretched out and his eyes were blank.

This wasn't happening. This couldn't be happening.

Jayne screamed, and staggered backward as the ghoul opened his mouth and spoke to her.

"I've been looking out for you, Jayne Jewell."

CHAPTER 25

Toby barked, standing his ground, his hackles raised. It would take more than the walking dead to scare him.

"Get back, get away," Jayne cried out as she took three steps back, her eyes still fixed on his face.

The corpse, the body, was coming for her—he was going to… Going to…

Then another part of her brain clicked into action. Why was the dead man so suntanned?

He wasn't pale and blue at all. In fact, he was a deep tanned bronzed colour, as if he'd been on a sunbed for too long.

But it was him. She was sure it was him! He'd come back to life, to haunt her, to follow her to kill her?

"Please, no. Don't kill me," she said, her voice coming out tight and strangled. She backed against a rock, almost falling over, struggling to keep her balance.

"I'm coming for you, Jayne Jewell," he said.

He was going to get her. No!

But something was wrong. His voice. It didn't have that charming local burr. His accent was odd. Not local at all.

Jayne stumbled backwards a little further, her eyes still fixed on his face.

Those dimples. The beard. It was him. But not the sun tan. Not that accent. It wasn't right.

More puzzled than scared now, she paused.

He held out his hand. It wasn't limp or pale, and the

fingertips weren't stained yellow.

None of this made sense.

"I'm Jago Jenkins. I hear you found my dead body."

She looked down at his outstretched hand. Her own hand moved forward to meet it.

On autopilot, Jayne shook his hand. 'I can't even refuse to shake hands with a corpse,' she thought, her sense of politeness too ingrained.

Would he hold her hand tight and pull her into the cold, cold water, under the waves until she drowned too, a corpse floating alongside his, in some terrible act of revenge?

To her utter relief, it was a strong handshake, the grasp firm and his skin reassuringly warm.

"You're not dead," she said, wonderingly, still not able to quite understand what was happening.

"You're not dead, are you?" she repeated, needing reassurance, still not making sense of it.

To her surprise, he laughed. It was a rich cheery bellow —not at all the sound a corpse would make, especially if it was trying to take her mortal soul.

"Well, yes and no. I'm going to my own funeral later, so I must be dead. That will be fun." He grinned at her, a devil-may-care smile full of mirth at the ridiculousness of the world. Was this how the devil drew you in?

"I don't understand. How? How is this possible?"

Toby meanwhile had decided that the man was no longer a threat, and was busily digging in the sand in between them. He flung sand up onto Jayne's legs. "Oh, Toby!" she exclaimed in mild irritation.

She was mid-meeting with a corpse that was following her around and reappearing with unpleasant regularity and Toby was interrupting with his digging.

The man looked down at Toby and laughed again. "He's

got a scent of something, and he won't let it go, not until he's satisfied. I know how he feels."

Jayne found herself feeling slightly giddy. The man—the dead man—was talking about her dog, making polite, pleasant conversation. How was this happening?

"Are you coming to my funeral later?" He smiled as if it was a lovely shared joke they had.

"Yes, of course," she answered. I need to pay my respects to... To you?"

"I thought I might hide in the hole and leap up just before they lower the coffin," he said. "That will give them all a fright."

Jayne frowned. "Yes. But the coffin might crush you first, and then where would you be? And why are you so suntanned? Have you been on holiday since...?"

She had been going to say, "Have you been on holiday since your death?" but that sounded utterly ridiculous. Perhaps he'd been in hell, and roasted by the fires there.

"I live in Australia. It's a lot sunnier than here."

"Yes, I hear it's very warm," she said, as if she was making small-talk at a party, rather than interrogating the dead man who seemed intent on talking to her. Well, that explained his accent.

"Yeah. It's great there. I wouldn't have come back. Except I heard that I'd died. And news like that makes a man curious, do you know what I mean?"

Jayne shook her head. "No. To be honest, I don't. Who are you? And what, exactly, is going on?"

"I'm waiting around down here out of sight. I don't want anyone to see me before the funeral. I don't want to spoil the surprise!" He clapped his hands with glee.

"So, you weren't waiting for me?"

"No. I'm just hanging about here. I caught the overnight train down from Paddington and walked here from Penzance. It was quicker than I expected, so now I'm just marking time until my funeral."

"But how did you know my name?" Jayne asked.

"I recognized you from the newspaper. That coat, and the dog. I knew it was Jayne Jewell, the body finder! I didn't mean to startle you. But when I saw you walking along the beach, I couldn't resist!"

Jayne frowned at him. It had been a cruel joke.

"I wanted to see if anyone would really think I was him." He chuckled merrily to himself.

"I'm not sure it *was* very funny," Jayne said, her tone rather acerbic.

He laughed louder. "You should have seen your face. It was like you'd seen a ghost. I hope the rest of them have the same reaction."

She really did think she'd seen a ghost—or even worse, a walking corpse come back to get her.

"Come on, sit down for a minute," he said.

Jayne knew she probably should be walking away from him. But her curiosity was far too strong and he didn't feel like a threat, not any more.

He was just a happy, suntanned man with a strong Australian accent—not at all what she had expected from a corpse.

She followed him around the rocks and sat down opposite him. The rock was smooth and warmed by the sun. She leaned down and patted Toby.

It was a lovely morning. Perfect for talking to a dead man, she thought wryly.

The apparition was looking around himself, smiling. "I didn't know how beautiful it is here. I should have come here years ago. Jimmy's got a lot to answer for."

"Explain yourself properly. Who are you? Who's Jimmy?

And what, exactly, is going on?" Jayne was getting slightly impatient.

"You're very demanding. I like that in a woman. Spirited. Feisty," he said.

She shook her head. "Don't flatter me, whoever you are. I've seen your dead body. I think I deserve an explanation as to how come you're suddenly alive again."

"Okay. I'll tell you. But only on one condition. You don't give away my secret until the funeral. I'm going to scare the pants off them all." He chuckled to himself again. "It's only an hour to wait. You can keep quiet until then?"

She nodded. Why not? It was his funeral after all.

CHAPTER 26

But he wasn't done yet. "Actually, there are two conditions. Can you fetch me something to eat? I'm starving."

Jayne agreed. "Yes. That's fine." At this point, she would agree to almost anything to find out who on earth this man was and why he was so intent on playing an unpleasant joke at his own funeral.

"Food first," he said. "If you go and get me something to eat and a cup of something hot, then I promise I'll tell you the whole thing."

Jayne briefly considered inviting the man to her apartment to wait until his funeral. But she heard Tabitha's voice very clearly, exclaiming in shock, 'You did what? You invited a strange man who might be dead into your apartment? Are you quite determined to do the most foolish thing in any given situation? Honestly, Mother!'

But the grocery shop was closed. The pasty shop is staying open, she remembered. "I can go and get you a pasty. They do tea and coffee too."

"Yes. Yes. A pasty. I've not had a proper Cornish pasty since Mum passed. She used to make them for us. And get me a coffee, please." He rubbed his hands together as if he was looking forward to it.

"Right. I'll be back shortly."

"Don't tell anyone I'm here. Don't let me down, Jayne. I know I can count on you," he called after her.

Jayne walked back up from the beach. In five minutes she

was outside the pasty shop. The smell made her feel slightly queasy, bringing back memories of the sea-sickness on the boat.

She tethered Toby outside and went in.

Mary Trelawney stood behind the counter. She looked even thinner and more waif-like than before.

"Oh. It's you. How are you?" Mary said.

"I'm fine, thanks. You?"

Mary shook her head. "I can't believe it's happening. Burying Jago. It doesn't seem real. I still keep expecting to see him walk in that door, as large as life and say, 'Give me your best pasty, Mary. You know I like them hot.' Oh!" She dissolved into tears and lifted her apron to dab her eyes.

"I'm so sorry for your loss. It must be so difficult." As she spoke the words, she wondered how Mary would react to seeing Jago leaping out at his own funeral.

Should she say something now, to prepare her? Or would it give the girl false hope, or unleash a barrage of questions to which she had no answer?

"We were going to get married. I didn't tell anyone. Hardly anyone. Everyone thinks I'm just 'one of his women.' And I'm not. We were going to be married." Tears rolled down her cheeks again.

"I'm so sorry," Jayne said again, feeling helpless. She needed to say something, about who she'd just met on the beach. But what?

A man pushed his way through from the back. "Mary. Calm down. It's about time you went anyway, if you will insist on going to that man's funeral."

Mary nodded wordlessly and untied her apron.

She disappeared into the back and the man stood in front of the counter. "She's upset. A close friend passed. He's being buried today. It's a difficult day for us all."

But he didn't look like he was finding it difficult. In fact, he seemed rather pleased with himself.

"Are you Mary's husband?" Jayne asked, knowing that he wasn't. She was just being nosy, but she couldn't resist.

"Brother," he replied shortly. "She's not married." He smiled broadly at Jayne, as if this was a good thing.

So he was a Trelawney and Mary's brother.

Jayne stared at him. Was he one of the pasty mafia she'd heard about? He didn't look like a gangster, just a well-fed, red-faced man in his forties.

Surely this man hadn't arranged the murder of his sister's feckless boyfriend? Or had he actually committed it?

Jayne didn't want to say anything about Jago to this pasty-mafia man. She would keep her mouth shut and let it play out as Jago—the new, living Jago—wanted it to.

"Now, what can I get you?"

"Oh. A large pasty."

"Large? Are you sure? They're big."

"Yes. I'm very hungry today," she said lamely. "And two coffees please. One with milk and sugar, the other just milk. I'm thirsty too," she said, then wondered why she'd bothered to explain that.

It wasn't exactly unusual for someone to buy two coffees, and this man had no idea that she was on her own.

She didn't know how the dead man took his coffee. But she guessed he'd be grateful for it however it came.

Mary's brother took a huge, almost twelve-inch long pasty from a tray behind him and put it in a paper bag. Then he made two coffees, the machine hissing and chugging.

Passing them to her, she paid and then struggled out of the shop. She put the pasty in her backpack, and balanced the coffees on the wall outside while she untethered Toby.

Then she sat down for a moment. She had to say something to someone. And she knew just the person.

Taking out her phone, she texted DCI Pollard. 'I don't know what's going on but someone calling himself Jago Jenkins is going to be at the funeral. I'm taking him a pasty now.'

She didn't know why she'd added that last part about the pasty. Was it relevant to anything? Not really, except to prove the man was alive and not imaginary—no phantom could eat their way through a large Trelawney's pasty.

A text message came back before she'd had time to pick up the coffees. 'I'll be at the funeral. Don't eat the pasties.'

She stared at the message. Well, she was pleased the Inspector would be at the funeral. That was good. He would see this new Jago Jenkins in the flesh. Texting him had surely absolved her of any collusion in the dead man's goings on.

But don't eat the pasties? Why not? The Inspector was no diet faddist. He'd positively encouraged her to eat chocolate cake when they'd been at that cafe. So why not the pasties? True, she wasn't tempted. Not after she was so sick last time.

"Oh Toby! He can't think that!" she exclaimed. Did the Inspector suspect she'd been poisoned? Had Mary, or that rather smug brother of hers, slipped something into her pasty that time? It would certainly explain the sudden unexpected onset of sea-sickness. She never got sea-sick. But she had been sick as a dog that morning. But why on earth would Mary have done that?

She'd seen Jayne down near what turned out to be Jago's cottage. Surely she hadn't jumped to the same conclusion as Kensa—that she, Jayne, was another of Jago's girlfriends?

But if she went around poisoning all the women he had had liaisons with, half the females in the town would be in their sick beds and the pasty business would have a terrible reputation.

Unless... Unless... Perhaps Jago *had* been faithful to Mary. Perhaps he had given up all other women. And when Mary saw Jayne at his cottage... Did she think Jayne was coming out of his house after a night together? Would that really be enough to make Mary try and poison her?

Her mind racing, Jayne made her way back along the High Street, a coffee in each hand and Toby's leash around her left wrist. One sniff of a seagull and he would pull away and she'd spill the coffee.

But for once, Toby was walking very nicely, close by her side, his nose lifting now and again to smell the delicious odours of the warm meaty pasty in her backpack. Perhaps this was the key to training him to be good—always carry a large, hot pasty in her backpack.

"I fed you some, and you were fine!" Jayne exclaimed, suddenly remembering.

A passer-by looked at her, startled.

"Sorry. I was just talking to my dog," Jayne explained as the woman hurried past her.

But even knowing yet another local had her down as a mad woman couldn't dent her delight. Mary hadn't tried to poison her. If she had, poor Toby would have been affected too. Thank goodness. It wasn't a nice thought knowing someone meant you harm.

If she wasn't a poisoner, perhaps Mary had knocked Jago out with a weapon of some sort—like a very large, well-baked pasty. She could feel the one she'd bought weighing her down. They really were like a brick. Was that what she'd done to Jago? Had she seen him with other women coming in and out of his cottage when she spied on him from her pasty-shop window, and then hit him with a large pasty to knock him out? No. Surely not. Perhaps her brother had done it.

But... But... Another thought was tickling away at the back of her brain, not quite ready to come forward.

Before she could focus properly, she was busy putting the coffees down, manoeuvring herself down onto the wall and then jumping rather heavily onto the sand.

She let Toby off his leash, relieved to have one less thing

to manage, and carried the coffees over to the other side of the jetty and beyond it to the rocks where the dead man Jago should be sitting and waiting, as large as life.

CHAPTER 27

As she approached the jetty, Jayne was filled with dread. What if... What if he was dead all over again?

She couldn't face seeing something so awful again.

Or trying to explain finding a third dead man to the disbelieving police.

She would be run out of town at this rate.

What if he just wasn't there at all and she'd imagined the whole thing?

With a sinking feeling, she remembered that she'd already texted the Inspector that he would be at his own funeral.

How would she live that down? The DCI would think she was mad, quite mad. And maybe she was, if she saw the dead coming back to life and asking for a pasty in a strong Australian accent.

Her stomach was tense and tight and her hands were almost shaking as she walked around the end of the jetty.

But there he was, alive and well and very much not imaginary!

He was sitting on the warm rock leaning back against the stone pier.

He raised his hand in greeting and smiled as he caught sight of the coffee cups.

Now, a dead man wouldn't do that, would they, Jayne reassured herself.

She quickened her pace.

"You're a sight for sore eyes." He held out his hand for a coffee and she set the other one down in the sand. Wrestling the pasty out of her rucksack, she passed it to him.

His eyes widened. "Now that's a pasty and a half! It's a good job—I'm starving."

Jayne sat down a few feet away from him and waited patiently as he munched his way through the gargantuan pasty.

Toby was digging happily at a random patch of sand, and the waves lapped against the shore.

'This is nice,' Jayne found herself thinking, as she sipped her coffee. Then she reminded herself what she was doing—about to attend the funeral of the man who was sitting near her, making short work of the massive pasty.

Once he'd finished, he rubbed his stomach. "Now, that was almost worth the journey from Australia," he said happily.

"So, tell me then. What's going on? Who exactly are you?"

"Jago Jenkins," he said happily. "As I live and breathe."

"Hmm. Not a very good choice of phrase for a man whose funeral starts in thirty minutes," Jayne said, checking her watch. "So, you're not the local ferryman? And you're not from around here?"

"No. And no. Well, my mum and dad were from here but I was born in Australia. Dad was a miner and when they all closed round here, he went out there. Loads of the miners did. They had me, and then things went wrong and when Little Jimmy came along, Dad knew Jimmy wasn't his kid. So he left. My new step-dad raised me. We were okay. But Jimmy…"

The man shook his head. "I don't know. We fought all the time. He was always jealous of me, I don't know why. He was better looking than me, cleverer than me, and taller too."

Jayne nodded, her mind racing. If Jimmy had been better looking than this man, he really must have been something.

Having only seen him when he was dead, and those

pictures of him in the newspaper, she thought they looked almost identical. But a taller, more handsome version? No wonder he set hearts fluttering wherever he went.

"Anyway, Jimmy left as soon as he was eighteen. Up and went and never kept in touch. We had no idea he'd left the country. But I guess he must have come here."

"But if his name was Jimmy, why did everyone call him Jago?" Jayne asked.

"I don't know. I'm pretty sure he took my passport, but why he used it instead of mine, I've got no idea."

"So you didn't know he lived here, using your name?"

Jago shrugged. "Not a clue. We didn't keep in touch. He made no effort to contact us and I didn't care if I never saw him again. And back then, there wasn't any social media or anything. Mum passed away a few years ago. I've been busy with my life. I've done okay for myself."

He took another drink of coffee, leaving the foam sitting on his top lip like a little moustache.

Then he grinned. "I tell you, it came as a bit of a surprise to hear I'd died. One of my friends, another Cousin Jack, saw it on some online news site."

"On Cornwall Today?" Jayne asked. She'd seen it too, the identical story to the one in the newspaper.

Jago grinned, laughing at the memory. "That's the one. You should have seen his face. He printed it off for me. He couldn't wait to tell me I was dead!"

"Surely, if he was your cousin, he knew it wasn't you?"

"Cousin? Oh, Cousin Jack. No, that's what they call all the Cornish miners out there. We're all Cousin Jacks down under." He laughed again, his tanned skin crinkling like paper. Then the smile faded.

"But of course it wasn't me. We all knew it wasn't me. Just a picture of me, more or less, and my name. I knew it had to be

Jimmy." He stared at the sea. "Mum's gone, I just found out Dad's been gone for years—years and years, and now Jimmy's gone too."

"I'm so sorry," she said. "It's hard when you lose someone you love." Her voice cracked, and she swallowed hard. This wasn't her grief.

He looked at her kindly. "True. Although, to be fair, there was no love lost between me and Jimmy. And I'd not seen my Dad since I was knee high and he left us and came back here. But I reckon little Jimmy got rich at my expense."

"How so?"

"I don't know if my Dad had anything when he died, but I think it all went to his only true son. Jago. And who was Jago? Little Jimmy, of course."

"So, your brother pretended to be you and inherited everything from your Dad?" She cocked her head to the side. Derek's voice popped into her head. 'Follow the money and find the motive.' Jayne's eyes widened. That would all be worth a pretty penny.

"Jimmy was born in Australia. No one even knew he existed, over here. And maybe he was clever enough to realise that. He had my passport. I suppose it's why no one ever contacted me when Dad passed away. They thought I'd been living here all this time—and dying here!"

"It must have been quite a shock."

"It still is. I can't quite take it in."

"Surely your father realised that Jimmy wasn't you?"

Jago shrugged. "He'd not seen either of us since we were little. I was just a kid and Jimmy was a baby when he left. And we look alike. I guess he was taken in, just like everybody else."

Jayne sat in thought for a few minutes, then a creeping feeling of dread overtook her. Follow the money and find the motive.

Who had a better reason for wanting Jimmy dead than the real Jago himself?

Had she been sitting with a man who'd killed his own half-brother in cold blood? Buying him a pasty and coffee?

Was she helping out a murderer?

CHAPTER 28

Jayne fumbled for her phone. She should call the Inspector right now. But of course she had no signal. Staring at her phone in despair she stood up.

She needed to get away from this man.

Misinterpreting her gesture, Jago started to get up too. "You're right. I should be going. Are you coming?"

"Where?" Jayne's mind had gone blank with fear. He was a murderer. She needed to get away.

"My funeral, of course! I can't wait to meet everybody!" He grinned happily.

Suddenly, she doubted herself. If he was a murderer, wouldn't he be hiding somewhere rather than making a public spectacle of himself?

The Church would be safe anyway, filled with people. She couldn't come to any harm there.

"I was planning on it. But is there time for me to take Toby home first and get changed?"

She cast another suspicious look at the hearty, bronzed man next to her.

He had the best motive, didn't he? Money was always a motive, and his younger brother had stolen what was rightfully his.

But, Jayne chewed her lip. Surely killing him was rather extreme. A visit to a lawyer would have been a better option. But tempers could run high. What if he'd confronted Jimmy and a fight had ensued and words exchanged and… Then he'd somehow drowned the poor man.

Jayne clipped the leash back on to Toby.

"There isn't time. Not if you want to see my grand entrance," Jago smiled at her.

She checked her watch again. She had planned on going home, dropping Toby off and changing into something more appropriate, but now she didn't have time, not now she'd met the dead man.

And she didn't want to lose sight of him either. Murderer or not, he's involved, she thought. He's a living, breathing clue. And one way or another, I'm involved in this too.

Toby would have to come with her. She had a feeling that with all the uproar this Jago seemed intent on causing, the presence of one small, occasionally well-behaved Jack Russell would be the least of anyone's concerns.

They walked along the coast path for a few minutes, hugging the side of the sea until they reached the bottom of the alleyway at the side of the Church.

Up at the top of it, Jayne could see people gathering, dressed in black.

She stopped and took off her raincoat, packing it into her rucksack. It was getting warm now anyway. Perhaps Tabitha had been right—it was rather brightly coloured. It certainly wasn't suitable for a funeral.

"Give me your scarf," Jago said suddenly.

"Why? Are you going to strangle me?" Jayne blurted out before she could stop herself.

He laughed, as if she was making an amusing quip, rather than revealing her darkest fears. "I want to hide my face."

She handed it over. It was a light cotton wrap in dark navy blue.

He spread it out and wrapped it around his face and neck.

He looked rather odd, especially with his beard emerging from the gap, but it did disguise him.

"Now, I'll wait down here, until they've all gone in. You nip up the alleyway, and wait at the top and then give me a signal when it's started. Then I'll make my entrance!"

Jayne wondered quite how she'd become an actor rather than a bystander in this plot of his.

But all the same, she made her way up the little narrow alleyway and onto the main road by the Church. The entrance was crowded with lots of people milling around.

She scanned their faces, recognizing Mary from the pasty shop. She looked different with her hair in a neat ponytail instead of bundled under a hair net. Her figure looking slender and girlish rather than waif-like now that she was wearing a fitted black dress, instead of being dwarfed by the bulky tabard she wore in the shop.

Nearby was Katie, the woman from the grocery store, her dark eyes darting around everywhere, taking everything in.

No doubt she's storing it all up for a good gossip later, Jayne thought, knowing that she was doing almost the same thing. But not for gossip, she told herself. For—for what? For finding out what on earth was going on in this strange little town.

Kensa was there too, her red hair washed and brushed and spilling down her back like a silky sheet of copper against her black cardigan.

The tall, handsome blonde man was there too. What was his name? Jayne was rather pleased she'd forgotten it—after all, he'd forgotten her almost immediately.

Mr Grumpy nodded at her and then resumed his baleful staring at the woman Jayne presumed was his ex-wife, Caroline. She looked very smart, in a short, tight black suit, black high-heeled shoes and even a little black pill-box hat pinned to her neat blonde hair.

Jayne tried to picture her in the rather scrawny, scruffy arms of Mr. Grumpy, but she couldn't quite make it work. Still, perhaps it's a case of opposites attracting, she decided.

DCI Pollard appeared at her side.

"Still alive then?"

She smiled at him, immediately feeling safer. "Yes. he's down there. The man I told you about." She inclined her head towards the alleyway. "I'm going to give him a signal when they've all gone in."

The Inspector frowned at her. "Give him a signal, hmm?" he looked as if he didn't quite approve—or as if he still wasn't entirely sure he believed her. "And you think he is who he says he is?" he asked.

She nodded.

"And you just met him quite by chance?"

Again, she nodded. "It's Toby. I have to walk down to the beach and around and about."

"Hmm. Still, you do seem to have a knack for finding this man, dead or alive."

His eyes remained fixed on hers and she was overcome with the urge to plead her innocence, to tell him how it really was all by chance and…

People started going into the Church. The Inspector moved away from her, joining another group, nodding politely to people, but glancing over at her every now and again.

Mr Grumpy called over to her. "Jayne. Are you coming in?" he said, as she lingered by the door.

"Not yet. The dog," she said.

He took it as a sufficient explanation and disappeared inside.

The Inspector remained outside, standing a few feet away from her.

"I'll tell him, now?" she said, almost as if she was asking the Inspector's permission.

"Give it a few more minutes. Let everyone get settled. I'll stand at the back. If what you say is true, I'm rather interested to see a few people's reactions to this."

Everyone was in the Church now, and Jayne could hear the Vicar speaking.

DCI Pollard slipped inside.

She went back to the alley. Jago was half-way up already.

She beckoned him on.

"I thought you'd forgotten," he grumbled. "Right. Let's see how dead I am!" He unwound the scarf from around his face and head, and smoothed his hair down.

"Here goes!" He gave Jayne a devilish grin and pushed open the doors of the church.

She couldn't resist following him in.

In the hushed, dimly-lit church, the Vicar was speaking. He was a tall, thin man with a pale face who looked like a cadaver himself, but he had a rich sonorous voice that boomed out, filling the space. He spoke warmly about the deceased, starting with his early life.

Jayne wondered how much of this was true—or if he was actually telling Jago's—not Jimmy's story.

Still, as his rather soothing voice, with its predictable rhythms continued, Jayne felt herself lulled into a strange peace. All eyes were turned to the front.

She felt Jago moving beside her. Would he wait and hear his entire eulogy?

But he wasn't waiting. He coughed loudly then called out, "G'day, everyone." His Australian-accented voice echoed through the church, overriding the Vicar's.

"I'm back!" he added, for good measure.

The Vicar stopped speaking.

As if they were controlled by a single impulse, every person turned around.

Jayne was confronted by a sea of faces.

Mary Trelawney screamed, the piercing sound rending through the shocked silence. Then other people cried out— some in shock at the interruption, others in fear at the return of the dead, and most just in plain disbelief at what was happening.

People scrambled from their seats, some backing away, others pressing forward, wanting to see the apparition close up.

"I'm real. I'm the real Jago Jenkins. And I'm alive!" he called out, clearly enjoying the reaction.

It was pandemonium.

Jayne stood back against the door, watching everything, amazed at how such a mournful, stately occasion had become a melee of noise and movement and chaos.

Mary sobbed and flung herself at Jago.

Apparently unsure how to handle it, he hugged her and patted her on the back, grinning round at everybody.

Others crowded around him, firing questions, reaching out to touch him as if to assure themselves he was actually real.

Kensa stood still in her pew, her red hair pushed back from her face, two red patches flushing her cheeks as she stared at Jago.

The tall blonde man hadn't moved either. He was at the other side, near the back, close to Jayne. His eyes were fixed on Jago—but then so were everyone's. His hand gripped the back of the pew tightly, his knuckles showing white. Why was he so annoyed? Had Jago stolen his wife too?

The Inspector moved through the crowd with practised ease and spoke to the Vicar.

The Vicar rapped on his lectern.

Silence fell for a moment and he leapt straight in. "I'm sorry to say that the funeral service of erm ..." He hesitated slightly... "Of the deceased will be postponed. I'm sorry for the abrupt change of schedule, but well, under the circumstances..." He glared at Jago. "If we could all vacate the church now, I'll be sure to let you know when we can resume proceedings. Thank you. Thank you."

The Vicar stepped down and began to usher people out, shepherding them from the front until the pressure and general flow of movement forced people out onto the street.

Jayne followed too, making sure Toby wasn't stepped on.

"I'm going to the pub. I need a few beers," Jago announced loudly.

He gave Jayne a smile as he passed, looking rather like the Pied Piper, with a trail of townsfolk following him, all wanting to find out the story.

CHAPTER 29

As the crowd thinned, Jayne moved closer to the inspector. "Aren't you going with him?" she asked.

He shook his head. "We'll pick him up shortly for a proper interview. Let him have his moment of glory. So, Jayne, with a y, do you want to tell me what's going on? First you bring me dead men, one after another and now a living one. I'm starting to think you might be more involved in this that you're letting on." He raised his eyebrows at her.

They need a trim, she thought, the irrelevant thought flicking through her mind as her mouth flapped open in dismay. "Involved? I hope you don't mean as a criminal of some kind. I can assure you that I'm perfectly innocent!" she insisted.

His face relaxed into a friendly smile. "I know. I know you are. I was just joking."

She closed her mouth, relief coursing through her. "Should you joke about things like that? In your position?"

He smiled again. "Probably not. But then again, I do quite a few things I'm not supposed to do. Like spending police expenses on coffee and cake. I hear they do a very good Victoria Sponge over there, if you fancy it?"

He gestured towards a cafe. A few tourists sat in there, easily recognisable by their brightly coloured clothes.

Jayne looked down at her own attire. Without her raincoat, she could almost pass for a local. If she added the obligatory fleece jumper, she'd be virtually indistinguishable.

"Umm, do they allow dogs inside?"

"There's a garden around the back. We could sit there."

Jayne followed the Inspector over the road. She went around the back of the cafe and found a delightful secret garden.

On three levels, it rose up behind the cafe, until the top level was higher than the houses and gave a wonderful view of the sea and St Michael's Mount. She chose a table right up at the top and sat down.

What was Jago Jenkins doing now? Was Mary still clinging to him? Would the poor woman have to grieve twice when she realised that he wasn't her fiancé come back from the grave, but another man entirely?

And what about the others? Mr. Grumpy, for example. How would he react? True, the real Jago Jenkins hadn't had an affair with his wife, but perhaps he still wouldn't be pleased to find the dead man so quickly replaced, especially by a man who was so similar in looks and attitude.

And Kensa. She'd looked both shocked and angry. Did she think that turning up at his own funeral was just another practical joke of Jago's? After all, unlike Jayne, Kensa hadn't actually seen Jago—or should she call him Jimmy now?—lying dead on the shore. For all Kensa knew, this could be another elaborate prank. Perhaps he'd been pulling annoying tricks all his life, getting attention, having a good laugh at other people's expense.

Jayne frowned in thought. Maybe that was why Kensa looked so cross—or perhaps she'd been secretly pleased to be rid of her philandering ex-husband and wasn't best pleased at the idea that he'd been somehow reincarnated.

The Inspector arrived, carrying a tray with two cups of coffee and two ample slices of Victoria Sponge cake.

The cake looked delicious. Jayne couldn't resist diving in. She took a large mouthful and sighed happily as she ate it. It was a light airy sponge, with a layer of fruity jam and just enough fresh cream in the centre to make it perfect. "You were right.

This is very nice."

DCI Pollard ate his with equal gusto. "I told you it was good," he said.

"But don't eat the pasties," she commented, remembering his rather odd instruction of earlier.

He cocked his head at her. "Ah yes. It was just a passing thought I had. Beware pasties. Cholesterol. Heart disease. All of that. It's good advice if you want to live to a ripe old age."

"But that wasn't what you meant, was it?" Jayne was puzzled now. "Cake is probably just as bad for you."

"I didn't want to alarm you—but your story about sudden sea-sickness stuck with me. It didn't seem quite right. And you'd just had a pasty, you said, handed to you by none other than the dead man's future wife. It just made me wonder, that's all."

"Ah. Now. You don't need to worry about the pasty. I know it was alright, because I gave half of it to Toby, and he was right as rain." Jayne felt rather pleased with her deduction, and knew the Inspector would be impressed.

"Ah, well. There you go. Another theory down the drain. I'll never solve the case at this rate." The Inspector looked entirely unperturbed by the thought, eating his cake contentedly and staring out to sea. "Marvellous cake. A marvellous view too. You never get tired of it."

"But you really think there's a case to solve?" Jayne said, her pulse quickening, refusing to be distracted by talk of the view. "You must do, if you thought Mary Trelawney had poisoned me."

The Inspector seemed to be very casual about the whole thing. Perhaps the idea of being nearly killed was quite a regular occurrence for him, but for her, it was something that demanded a little more discussion.

He turned back to her. "You saw the body. It disappeared. You ate the pasty. You were uncommonly sick. It's an odd coincidence. Did you have any other symptoms that morning?

Or did anything else strange happen?"

"Well, I know this will sound silly but..." Should she tell the Inspector about seeing sharks and dead men?

"Tell me. Sometimes it's the peculiar little details, the 'silly' things, as you say, that can make or break a case."

"So it *is* still a case," she said, feeling vindicated—and rather smug that she'd caught the DCI out in a slip of the tongue. "The newspaper said you had ruled it an accidental death, but you haven't, have you?"

He shrugged, giving her a half-smile, as if he knew he'd said too much. "The police don't rule it anything. That's not our job. The Coroner will do that, and it won't be discussed in the Coroner's court for another week or two. And you can't believe everything you read in the newspapers. But sometimes it helps if people think there's no suspicion. They get comfortable—and make mistakes."

Jayne leaned forward, wiping a crumb from her mouth. "You do think he was murdered?" She tried not to sound excited, but she didn't quite manage it.

"Let's say that it's still a matter of interest. Hence my presence at the funeral. I would have attended anyway, but after I got your text, I certainly wasn't going to miss it. And of course, I need this informal interview with a potential witness." He smiled at her. "And some rather good cake."

Jayne smiled back. She was a potential witness in a criminal case. And it was still a matter of interest. That was good enough.

"So, tell me. What 'silly' things happened that morning?"

"Oh. I just felt rather odd. I was light-headed, disorientated really. I kept seeing things. I'm sure it was just the shock. I saw his face. And sharks in the water." She felt idiotic saying it, but he wanted to know everything.

"Sharks, hmm?" He regarded her steadily. "It's a good job Jefferies didn't note that down too. But this wasn't immediately after you'd seen the body?"

"No, no. I'd been back to the apartment, got changed, had the pasty of course, and bought my tickets for the Mount online. Then we'd gone down to the boats, me and Toby. It was only then that I started feeling very odd. And then I was sick. Properly sick, right over the side of the boat. And for the rest of the day, I felt strange, thirsty, dizzy, and just very, very odd really."

He nodded. "It's unlikely that it was sea-sickness. That usually resolves as soon as you're on dry land again. And you don't strike me as a particularly fanciful woman. Artistic, perhaps, but not the type to imagine things like that."

"I never have done before," she said. This wasn't the time to tell the Inspector that Derek still spoke to her quite frequently, and that she often heard Tabitha's voice berating her about something or other. But maybe everyone had that—the voices of their nearest and dearest in their heads. It wasn't as if she actually thought it was real. Not really. No.

"Is there anything else about that morning?"

His question dragged her back into the moment. She thought for a second, wondering if there was anything. "Well, the boat man and his assistant were talking about Jago. Jimmy. About how he should be sacked. I got the feeling he was skimming money off the top, and they moaned that he was always missing work."

The Inspector took a drink of coffee and carefully dabbed the foam from his upper lip. "Yes. The issues with the boat are known to us. In fact, there was a planned investigation into it. But that's small stuff. And if anything, Jago should have been bumping off the people who were trying to get him sacked, not the other way around. No. Something happened. An inciting incident. Something that made someone believe they had to act quickly—and definitively. Someone who had a lot to lose if Jago —or Jimmy—stayed alive. Now, who could that be?"

He stared out at the view for a few moments.

"His brother. The real Jago," Jayne said, suddenly certain that she'd solved the case. "It has to be him, doesn't it? I mean, it sounds like Jimmy stole his identity and his whole life really. There's got to be a reason for that. And surely it's enough to drive anyone to murder? It's almost like he murdered himself! Perhaps he thought he could kill Jimmy and then just take his place and no one would notice. They really do look alike."

The Inspector took another drink of coffee, leaving Jayne's suppositions hanging in the air. She was momentarily annoyed. Shouldn't he be leaping up, exclaiming, 'That's it. You've cracked the case!' But he just sat there, enjoying his coffee for a minute.

Then he shook his head. "Flight records are easily checked. I had someone look them up as soon as I heard him speak at his funeral. He's clearly Australian. He didn't arrive in the country until several days after the news article was published. The man on the beach had been dead for a week by then. It's highly unlikely that this man had any involvement in the death. And if he really is who he says he is, all he needs to do is go to a decent solicitor to prove his identity. There's no need to kill Jimmy. Again, it would make a lot more sense for Jimmy to kill him, if there was any killing to be done between them."

"Perhaps he did. Perhaps Jimmy was Jago all along and Jago was Jimmy and now this one—the live one—has tricked us about who he is. Think about it. He's really Jimmy. He kills his older half-brother and pretends he was Jago all along!"

The Inspector smiled. "You'll make an excellent novelist, but no, I don't think that theory will fly for a police investigation. Again, the flight records show that whoever he is, he wasn't in the country when his brother died. If he was in Australia, as he says, and that is very easy to check too, then he can more than likely be ruled out. Unless he was in league with someone here." The Inspector seemed to consider it briefly then shook his head. "The simplest solution is usually the most likely. We humans are not very complex creatures on the whole."

Jayne felt rather deflated. This investigating lark wasn't as easy as she'd thought. Logic seemed to go against all her best ideas. But perhaps murder wasn't logical? Derek said follow the money, but perhaps anger and passion got in the way too.

She finished her cake, saving a little piece for Toby. He'd been giving her the side eye the whole time she'd been eating—looking at her plate, then at her, then away, as if he was trying to watch her without her knowing.

She smiled and fondled his head. Life was simple for Toby. He didn't worry about motives or money or anything like that. A piece of cake? Happy as anything. A walk outside? Delighted. She slid her plate down under the table, and watched as he licked it. It was terribly unhygienic, of course, but surely the cafe would put it through the dishwasher anyway?

"So, if it wasn't the brother, what did happen?" she asked.

The Detective Chief Inspector smiled at her. "We might never know. There's only one thing making me think it was foul play—and that's you. Seeing the body the first time, and knowing someone had to have moved it."

"Why, though? If he drowned, he drowned. What did it matter *when* it was found?" she asked.

"My thinking entirely. There's a reason for it. Whoever he was, Jimmy or Jago, there's some reason why he was killed on that day and not a week or a month earlier or later, and some reason why his body was moved. If someone killed him, they wanted him to be discovered a few days later, and not that very morning. But why?" The Inspector fixed his quizzical gaze on her, and Jayne felt rather like she used to when she was in school and she was asked for the answer to a particularly hard maths problem.

Her mind was devoid of solutions.

She tried to look like she was having all kinds of good ideas and thinking really hard about it, but actually she needed the loo. She had drunk two large coffees and had been out for hours.

She couldn't wait any more. She stood up. "I'll be back in a moment. Would you watch Toby for me?" she said.

Toby seemed perfectly content to sit with the DCI.

That's a good sign, Jayne thought to herself. Toby must trust him.

I do too, she thought. And it seems like he trusts me too.

CHAPTER 30

On her way back up the three flights of stone steps, she began to wonder why she'd selected the top terrace.

Trying not to puff too much, she paused for a moment, admiring the flowers. They were those lovely Angel's Trumpets. The stems looked rather like a succulent. They'd root easily, she thought, glancing around.

A young couple were sitting at a table nearby, but they were deeply engrossed in conversation, their hands entangled over the table, their eyes locked on to each other.

Perfect, Jayne thought, my romantic hero and heroine will do that too—and be just as unaware of what is happening around them.

No one else was around. Jayne slid out her hand and snapped off the end of a piece of the plant.

Slipping it into her pocket, she carried on up to the top terrace.

She could try and get it to root, and then plant it up and keep it in her conservatory back in Hertfordshire, and nurture it into a lovely plant, a fitting souvenir of her holiday.

As she sat down, she thought about hiding the plant in her rucksack. The Inspector wouldn't notice, would he? She pulled her bag onto her lap. "I'll just see if I've got a treat for Toby," she said, and unzipped the bag.

"I'll pop this in," she murmured, hoping he was looking out at the view and taking no notice of her.

"What's that?"

His voice made her freeze.

His casual, relaxed tone had disappeared and he sounded quite fierce.

She dropped the plant into her bag. "Nothing. Nothing. Just a flower. I picked it. It's nothing." But her heart was pounding.

My Goodness, she thought, I am not cut out for a life of crime.

Guilt was flooding through her and she could actually feel her face flushing.

He passed her a paper serviette. "Take it out of your bag. Use this. Don't touch it," he said.

His voice was so authoritative that she obeyed him instinctively. "But it's just a flower, a little cutting," she said.

Taking the paper, she pulled out the evidence of her crime. He was taking this too seriously. Was he making her use the serviette so she wouldn't disturb her fingerprints? Because this was evidence?

Her stomach twisted in an anxious knot. Evidence. Of a criminal offence. Theft.

Tabitha would never forgive her. What had she been thinking, stealing something when she was having coffee with an actual real-life police officer?

She put the plant down on the table, using the paper napkin as instructed. "I'm sorry. I know I shouldn't have taken it. But I thought I could grow it on. Just as a little souvenir, that's all. Look, I'll take it down to the cafe and apologise and offer to pay for a new plant. Really. I don't know what I was thinking. I'm so sorry."

Inspector Pollard looked at her, still frowning. "That's not what I'm worried about. It's this damn plant. They shouldn't be growing it here at all. Go and wash your hands—now. And be thorough. Very thorough."

Puzzled, Jayne stood up. Leaning down to give Toby a reassuring stroke, she was startled upright again by the Inspector's curt voice.

"Don't touch him. Don't touch anything—not until you've washed your hands thoroughly. And I mean thoroughly. As if you're about to perform surgery."

Jayne trotted back down the steps, holding her hands out in front of her as if she was Lady Macbeth. "Unclean, unclean," she murmured to herself.

Better to be unclean than to be arrested for theft or criminal damage or something. But the Inspector was going over the top, wasn't he?

Some plants did have sap that could be an irritant, that was for sure, but she'd only touched the stalk.

"Back again?" the waitress said as Jayne walked near the counter to the bathrooms.

"Oh, yes. I just need to wash my hands," Jayne said.

Fortunately, there was a sink outside the toilets. She stood there, soaping her hands up and washing them, then rinsed them off. Then she remembered how insistent the Inspector had been, and began to wash them again.

"Out, out, Damned spot," she murmured, rubbing soap into her palms and between her fingers.

The waitress was watching her out of the corner of her eye.

Jayne stopped talking to herself. Just because it was Shakespeare, it wouldn't stop people thinking she was odd and she'd had quite enough of people assuming she was slightly unhinged.

"OCD?" the waitress asked, a sympathetic smile on her face. "My aunt does that. She washes her hands red-raw sometimes."

Jayne just smiled in response. She could hardly say that she was washing her hands so thoroughly because she'd stolen a plant from their garden.

She made her way back up to the terrace. This time when she stopped for a breather halfway, she didn't give in to her urge to take a little cutting of any of their lovely tropical-looking plants.

Sitting down again, she saw the Inspector regarding her cutting as if it might leap up and go for his throat.

"It's Angel's Trumpets. They are glorious flowers. I just thought I might try and grow it at home. It's very rare. Quite tender, I expect. I really shouldn't have taken a little cutting," she said, trying to minimise her act of criminality.

"No. You shouldn't have done. But not because it's criminal—well, it's probably on the edge of being legal. But because it's poisonous. Very poisonous."

Jayne's mouth fell open. "Really? But it looks so beautiful."

"Hmm. We've had some issues with it in the last few years. This is Brugmansia. It looks nice, but in this case its common name has a double meaning. They are Angel's Trumpets that really will send you to heaven, if you're not careful."

She looked at him. That reminded her of something. "Staring blankly up at the heavens," she said.

"Hmm. You will be if you have too much of this. Unfortunately, it makes you high. We had some trouble a while back. It was growing in the local park in Penzance and some of the youth started picking it and using it for recreational purposes. But it can kill you. Several of them ended up in hospital, quite ill. They removed it from the public parks, of course and there was a campaign to stop people growing it, but evidently not everyone listens."

"I'll be alright though, won't I? I only touched it a little." Jayne was suddenly relieved she'd followed the Inspector's instructions about washing her hands very carefully.

He nodded. "Yes. To be honest, you have to ingest the seeds or leaves, or brew it up, to get the full effect. Then you can have anything from euphoria to hallucinations to a coma and even death. Extreme thirst, heart irregularities. All sorts of fun, according to the youth of today. I don't know why they would risk it."

Jayne frowned. Extreme thirst, Hallucinations. Sharks? "How about vomiting?"

"I would recommend it if you'd eaten it. It's the only way to get it out of your system. Induce vomiting, or use a stomach pump. But you don't need to worry. I was being overcautious. I wouldn't like to take you out for a coffee and have you end up being poisoned." He smiled at her, his good humour seeming to return.

But Jayne didn't feel quite so relaxed. "No. I mean… You said that can cause hallucinations? You remember that I told you I was ill, before—sea-sick and light headed and confused?"

The Inspector regarded her steadily. "I do. I do indeed. And I suspected the pasty. But it would be hard to eat this plant without knowing it. I suppose seeds could have been baked into the pasty."

"How do people usually take it?" Jayne was starting to feel slightly sick.

"Tea, I believe. They boil up the seeds and leaves and make a tea."

"I had tea. At Kensa's cottage. After I saw the body. While I was waiting for the police officer, for Officer Jefferies. She made me tea. I thought it tasted odd. But… But…" Jayne left the thought hanging. Had she really been in danger? It didn't bear thinking about.

The Inspector had that rather intense, fierce look on his face again.

Somehow that made Jayne feel worse. She wanted him to

smile and dismiss her concerns with a light-hearted comment, reassuring her that she was being silly.

But she knew from his face that she was being entirely sensible. "Was I poisoned?" she asked.

He tapped the teaspoon on his saucer. Tap, tap, tap.

"It's far too late for toxicology. But it sounds possible. You ingested the tea. Then you vomited. But still felt unwell for a few hours after that. You say you had hallucinations? Euphoria?"

She pushed her coffee cup away. She didn't feel like drinking the rest of it now. "Mild hallucinations. I thought it was just the shock. Or just me being silly. I saw his face. The sharks in the water. But not euphoria."

"You did decide to set off for the Mount, despite the difficult morning you'd had," he said. "Was that entirely in character?"

She shrugged. "I suppose I did feel excited to be here and I wanted to explore. Yes, maybe I should have been taking it easy, given what had happened, rather than insisting on going over on the boat."

"But perhaps it saved you. A combination of Angel's Trumpets, a heavy pasty and the motion of the boat made you unwell. Vomiting is rarely pleasant, but in this case, it could well have saved your life."

He held her gaze and she knew then how serious it had been.

She had been genuinely close to being poisoned. If she'd stayed at home, in her room, anything could have happened.

If it wasn't for the motion of the boat making her unwell, and giving her a kind of do-it-yourself stomach pumping, she would have absorbed all of the poison.

Tabitha was far away, and she didn't know anyone else here. She would have been alone in her apartment.

She could have just... gone.

She stroked Toby's head, loving how soft his ears were. Oh Toby. What would have happened to him if she'd slipped into a coma and died?

"The Angel's Trumpets, blowing me up to heaven," she said softly.

"Indeed. Indeed. But they didn't. You're still here and very much alive."

CHAPTER 31

Later that day, Jayne left Toby at the apartment for a few hours.

She had to go into Penzance and make an official statement. The Inspector had insisted, given the new information that had come to light.

Relieved it wasn't Jefferies on duty, she sat in front of two Police Officers and went through the entire story again. From waking that day, taking Toby out, talking to Kensa, admiring the Angel's Trumpets growing outside her door, seeing the body, and then everything that happened afterwards too.

The officers asked a lot of questions about Kensa's cottage, the tea, the phone calls. "We logged a call from Kensa Jenkin's at 7.58. Officer Jefferies was there within twelve minutes. His notes show that clearly. There's no traffic at that time and he left immediately when the call was made. We don't get many reports of dead bodies, so he was fast. Despite Ms. Jenkin's insistence on the phone that you were, quote, 'a raving lunatic,' and 'a tourist who doesn't know what's going on.' "

Jayne felt really quite cross. No wonder Jefferies hadn't taken her seriously.

"Well, it was a lot longer than twelve minutes. I can't say how long, but she made a phone call, then made me some tea, then went off for a while. Her phone rang too. Someone called Dave. It was much more like thirty or forty minutes until Officer Jefferies showed up. I was starting to worry that no one was going to come."

They made notes, smiling at her, encouraging her to talk, but not saying much else.

"Dave. Yes. We'll look into that. Tell us more about the tea, and the kitchen."

Jayne described it as clearly as she could. Her memory was slightly hazy but there were certainly saucepans of gunky stuff on the stove, messy plates and mugs all around, the bundles of coloured paper. "Ferry tickets!" she exclaimed, suddenly realising where she'd seen them before. The boat assistant had a roll in her hand, and tore one off for every passenger.

She told them about the ticket on the sand too, and how she still had it.

More questions followed, about her ill-fated trip over to the Mount, her symptoms, everything.

She even told them how surprised Kensa had seemed, next time they'd met.

The officers duly noted everything down, and the voice recorder's red light glowed throughout, keeping her statement for posterity.

Then she told them about meeting Jago—the living Jago —on the beach and what he'd said about his half-brother Jimmy and Australia, and everything she could remember."

But they didn't tell her anything, or confirm any of her suspicions, or even let on if she was saying anything useful.

"Thank you. We'll look into it," was all they would say.

At the end of the interview, one of them said, "We may want to talk to you again. And if this comes to anything, you may be called as a witness. Therefore, I would advise you to have no contact of any kind with Kensa Jenkins or anyone else close to her. Perhaps it might be better to return to..." The Officer consulted his notes. "Hertfordshire."

Jayne felt heavy-hearted. She still had a week left of her

holiday. "I'm not sure I'm ready to go back just yet. Do I have to?" she asked.

"Not at all. You are free to do as you wish. But be careful. Don't accept drinks from strangers, or people you've just met. You could be the crucial witness in this case, Ms. Jewell. So, be careful."

She left the Police Station and walked down the High Street. There were lots of charity Shops, a lovely book shop, cafes, pasty shops. It was all very pleasant—but the stroll through the charming town was coloured darker by her thoughts. She glanced at everyone as if they were out to get her, suddenly wary and suspicious.

The police warnings were still ringing in her ears. Was she actually in danger? Reaching the bottom of the town, she paused at the bus station.

She could get on the bus, or walk all the way back to Marazion along the coastal footpath. But walking didn't seem right without Toby.

She decided on the bus.

She was a crucial witness, she thought to herself. She had to 'Be Careful.' It almost sounded like Tabitha speaking. Be careful. Be wary of strangers. Good advice, perhaps. Certainly now, it was very good advice. "I will be careful, Tabby, don't worry," she said under her breath as pressed the bell to indicate to the bus driver that she wanted to get off at the next stop.

Even though the police hadn't shared any details with her, Jayne knew. She could work it out herself.

Kensa hadn't called the police. She'd called someone else. And that could only be to move the body. And that could only be because Kensa knew exactly who was dead and she didn't want him found. And she would only know he was dead if she'd had a hand in killing him.

But *why*? Why kill the man who provided her with a home, whether he was Jago or Jimmy? And why care when his body was found, if he was already dead?

As she climbed down the steep steps of the bus into the little town square, she looked around cautiously. No. There was no one waiting to attack her. There was no one much around at all, except a few tourists already queueing at the fish and chip shop.

She was safe.

CHAPTER 32

Anna was closing up her shop and waved to her.

Jayne went over for a chat.

"How's the knitting coming along?"

"Fairly well. It's a lovely pattern. It's more complicated than anything I've done for a while but I'm enjoying it. It's a challenge, you know?" To be honest, that could go for her entire holiday so far.

"Great. Are you busy later? I'm meeting up with a few of the other knitters this evening at the pub to compare progress. It's supposed to be a knitting circle but to be honest, there's more Cabernet than cable-knit." Anna laughed. "And there was a lot of drama today. We're just dying to get together and have a chat about it! You wouldn't believe what's been going on here!"

Jayne nodded eagerly. She would believe it. She really would. But, 'dying' to get together? Surely Anna wasn't a risk? Was she in on it too? Jayne tried to get a grip. Of course she wasn't. She was being paranoid.

An evening in the pub, talking about knitting and the strange events of the funeral were just what she needed. "I don't suppose I can bring Toby?"

"Your husband?" Anna looked surprised. "Well, we don't normally invite partners but…"

"No. No." Jayne laughed. One dead man risen from the grave was quite sufficient. She didn't need Derek reappearing too. He was present enough as it was, always in her head.

"My dog. Remember? You met him before. My little terrier. It's just he's been at home all afternoon because I—" She stopped, not sure if she should say where she'd been. "I went into Penzance," she finished.

"Oh sure. Bring him. He's adorable. I bet he's less trouble than a husband too!"

Jayne smiled at her quip. Anna didn't know Jayne was a grieving widow. But why would she? Jayne wasn't acting like one. In fact she hadn't really felt like one since she'd been here. Perhaps the holiday, strange as it had been, was working.

It was the first chapter of the next stage of her life. It wasn't a stage she'd ever wanted, or hoped for, but it was here and so she had to make the best of it.

Derek wouldn't mind. He hated moping and wasting time. He'd been quite clear on that. "You get on with your life, Jayne, when this is over. Don't waste it, just because I'm not around. I'll be watching you!" He'd been light-hearted at the time, and she'd laughed at the idea.

This was before, when his death was inevitable but still far enough away to be discussed lightly. But now it had happened, she felt he really was watching her. And maybe, just maybe, he'd be pleased.

"Who else will be there?" She had suddenly remembered the warning of the Police Officers.
Anna reeled off a few names. There was Mary from the Pasty shop, Katie from the grocery store and two others that Jayne didn't recognize. "There aren't very many. And we're all friendly. We don't bite," she smiled.

"How about Kensa Jenkins?" Jayne felt she had to ask.

Anna gave her a rather puzzled look. "No. No. She's not part of the circle. She's… not." Anna trailed off, as if there was something she didn't want to say.

Jayne nodded, not explaining the reason for her question. Knitting. The pub. And Toby could come too. That would be nice.

Back at her apartment, Jayne was greeted rapturously by Toby, who acted as if she'd been away for months rather than just a few hours. She took him out for a quick walk and then settled into her chair overlooking the sea.

"Now, how about a nice cup of tea and I might just write for a while," she said to Toby.

He lay on the floor at her feet, his eyes closing. Perhaps he found her romance ideas tiresome. But if she was ever going to get her book written, she would have to get on with it.

She flicked back through her pages of notes. She had quite a few snippets now. It wouldn't be long before she could start properly. Her characters were coming together and a plot was forming in her mind.

Perhaps the hero would be a Cousin Jack, toiling at the coal face, coming out blackened and sweaty, and the heroine would wash him down with a wet cloth.

No. No. That's straying a little into rather tempestuous territory. But all the same, a miner for her hero? It could be a good idea. She'd had enough of seafaring folk for now.

She settled at the table, overlooking the bay, sipped her mug of tea and spent a very pleasant while jotting down scenes and ideas. They were all rather exciting, with her tanned handsome miner, coming up from the ground like some Earth God, all muscles and dirt.

Then she paused. Was dirt romantic? Could he grip the heroine with his blackened hands? Or would he just leave messy marks on her clothes that she would have to wash out by hand? After all, she wouldn't have a washing machine, not back in those days. She would be rather irritated, and snap at him to keep back if he tried to embrace her with coal-blackened hands.

But they didn't mine coal in Cornwall, did they?

She did a quick search online. No. No coal. Lots of tin. Silver. Copper. And now Lithium.

Hmm, what would a miner look like as he emerged from a tin mine? Shiny silver, like the tin man in the Wizard of Oz? Of course not. How about lithium? But that sounded far too modern and to be honest, she wasn't entirely sure what it was.

Oh dear. She really needed to do some more research. Perhaps a fisherman was easier. But too fishy.

Perhaps her hero would emerge just a little hot and dirty. His muscles rippling, his biceps bulging, the sweat dripping down his bare chest. Or was it cold down there in the Cornish mines? And he wouldn't be tanned of course, not if he spent every day underground. He would pale and cold and perhaps a little clammy.

The memory of the dead man swam into her mind.

She tried to push the vision of the dead body away again and focus instead on the very much alive, and really quite attractive brother from Australia.

Would he be in the pub again tonight, holding court and still shocking everyone with tales of how he was the real Jago Jenkins?

Jayne put her pen down. Her hero was all muddled up with the dead man and his brother and she needed to get them both out of her mind if she was to clear her head. Now, what about the tall blonde man? Would he do as the hero?

What was his name again? She rustled in the fruit bowl, digging beneath the two apples and a blackening banana to find the business card he'd left with her.

Daniel. Daniel David Penhaligon. Now that was a nice name. And he had been a nice man, if rather superficial. But she could still model her hero on him.

And the girl. Maybe Mary, with her slender frame and pale, mournful face. And Kensa was the vengeful other woman. The poisoner. The killer.

Mary. Daniel. Kensa. Hmmm.

But no killers please, this was supposed to be romance, lovely and passionate, yes, scary and fatal—no.

"The problem is, the real actual people keep getting in the way, and I just can't seem to get a grip on my characters," Jayne said to Toby. "No. I'll leave it for now. Dinner, a short walk, and then the pub. How about it, boy?"

Toby jumped to his feet, wagging his tail enthusiastically. Jayne realised she'd made a critical error, mentioning the w-word before it was time for the actual w.

"Dinner first." She looked in the fridge for something to distract him with.

She found some cheese and made him sit before she fed him a few morsels. There. That had taken his mind off the walk for long enough for her to make dinner and then gather up her knitting and go.

She would take Toby for a stroll on the way to the pub.

A walk was a good tonic for everything—grief, boredom, loneliness, or even pondering on the thorny problem of whether Kensa really killed the fake Mr. Jago Jenkins and why.

CHAPTER 33

Soon enough, Jayne was settled in the pub. Toby was at her feet, quite content now he'd had his evening ramble. She sat next to Mary with Anna across the table and Katie and two other women there too.

Katie was busy looking around, commenting on everything that was going on.

"Who's she glaring at?" Katie said. "Look. It's Kensa. Is it you, Mary? Why is Kensa looking at you like that? And Caroline too. It can't be you, Jayne, can it? Surely you've not been here long enough to upset the precious Kensa?"

Jayne smiled tightly. Kensa and Caroline did seem to be glaring at their table. After the police warnings earlier, Jayne was glad she was surrounded by friends and not having to face Kensa alone.

"It's you, Mary. Oh, of course. Because of him. I get it," Katie said, offering Mary a sympathetic smile. "But I don't know why that's making Caroline stay away. She usually enjoys our knitting evenings."

Anna laughed. "But haven't you noticed, since she left her husband, she's been getting kind of fancy-looking. Maybe knitting doesn't fit her new image."

"You could be right," Katie said. "She does look a lot more glamorous than she used to. But that doesn't explain why she's looking at us like that."

Jayne thought she might know. But she didn't want to tell anyone that her name could have been linked in a romantic way to Caroline's ex, Mr. Grumpy himself.

It was a complete misunderstanding, without any basis in truth, and Jayne didn't want to add any more fuel to the fire by telling Katie that she'd been out for a drink with him, or become neighbourly friends.

Before Anna or Katie could continue the subject, Jayne excused herself. "Let me go and get some drinks," Jayne offered. "To say thank you for inviting me. I really appreciate it."

She took their orders and went up to the bar. As the newcomer to the group, it was right to establish herself as a full, paying member, rather than just a hanger on.

She didn't want to admit that her real reason for offering was more selfish. After talking to the police today, she was happier drinking something she had sourced herself.

She nodded to Kensa but she was still glaring at their table. Caroline was standing behind her, and she gave Jayne a fierce, sneering look.

"Damn tourists," Caroline observed loudly. "Pushing their way in and thinking they own the place. Even when they look like that."

Caroline turned her back and Jayne sighed. She'd certainly made an enemy there. But it wasn't her fault. She genuinely had not one iota of interest in this woman's husband. But she couldn't suppress just one tiny hint of smugness at being thought of as a love rival.

With her sleek blonde bob and her well-maintained nails and nicely made-up face, Caroline obviously put a lot more effort into her looks.

It must be galling to think you've had your man seduced by a woman in a green and yellow anorak.

Jayne tried to smile as she listened to Kensa's rather gruff reply. She did have quite a husky voice for a woman. And big shoulders.

A thought was coming to her, wandering about in the depths of her mind, like her thoughts tended to these days.

Once, when she was young, her ideas had come thick and fast, unprompted. Now it was sometimes like trying to squeeze the last piece of toothpaste from the tube.

She knew it was in there but it didn't want to come out.

"Wake up, lady. Do you need help?" the girl behind the bar said.

"Mad as a hatter," Kensa muttered, to no one in particular.

Oh my. They were talking to her—and about her. She had been miles away, trying to pin down that errant idea.

She looked up to find Kensa glaring at her, and Caroline smirking.

The barmaid was polishing a glass, looking at her with increasing concern.

Barmaid? Was that an okay term anymore? Maybe she should ask Tabitha—she was forever snapping at Jayne telling her she 'couldn't say that anymore.'

Anyway, the person serving the drinks. The bartender. That had to be okay, didn't it? Life was so complicated now, she sighed. If she ever wrote her book, Tabitha would likely go through it with a red pen like an angry teacher, striking out all her outdated and accidentally insulting phrases and terms.

"Sorry. I was just daydreaming," Jayne said brightly. "Don't mind me. But I do want some drinks."

She placed the order, making sure she got it right, and tried not to gasp at the amount it came to. 'Costs and benefits, Jayne,' she heard Derek say. 'You rarely have one without the other.'

It was certainly a benefit to feel part of a group like the knitting circle. Friendship, a common interest and their propensity to gossip were all most welcome at the moment.

Watching carefully, she kept her eye on the wine bottle,

following it from shelf to opening through to being placed in front of her.

There was no possibility of it being interfered with. Being the victim of a potentially fatal poisoning had made her wary now.

She took the bottle of wine and a bottled lager back to the table, then returned to the bar for the other drinks.

New Jago—the real Jago—had arrived in the bar. He was clearly already very at home there.

Kensa was laughing at something he was saying.

Jayne shrugged to herself. If she'd fallen for Jago Mark One, there was no reason not to find Jago Mark Two attractive.

"Of course, you've got to be nice to me. I'm your landlord now. I suppose if I hadn't turned up, you'd have got the whole damn lot, still being his wife. You must have been gutted when I arrived."

Jayne didn't catch Kensa's mumbled answer, but the thought stayed with her.

When she sat down again, Jayne paused for a moment. Poor Mary looked forlorn and pale and on the edge of tears. Her eyes kept flickering to the new Jago, as if he was a continual reminder of what she'd lost.

It would be cruel to ask her now. But Jayne had to know.

The conversation flowed for a while, touching on the funeral and the shock, but veering away again.

The women were clearly making a concerted effort to keep Mary's mind off recent events.

They talked about knitting, but even that wasn't safe ground. "I was knitting it for him!" Mary exclaimed. "For my Jago." She put her bundle of wool and needles into her lap and gave in to tears.

Jayne joined in the communal sympathising and reassuring. But then she thought, 'Oh well. The poor girl is already in tears. I can't make it much worse.'

She patted Mary's hand. "Was your Jago still married to Kensa?"

Mary shrugged and wiped tears from her cheek, casting a baleful glance across the bar. "In name only. They'd been separated for years, but they just never made the split official. He was going to do it, the Monday before they found him. He was going to file for divorce and then go and see my brothers and make everything right. That's why they didn't like him. Because he had a reputation and he was still married to someone else. But he was going to do the right thing. He'd settled down, he really had."

"How unfortunate. Oh, Mary. I'm so sorry. I lost my husband, but we knew that was coming. I can't imagine the shock you felt."

Mary gripped her hand, the knuckles showing white.

But under her concern, other questions were pressing forward and Jayne had to ask. "So, did your Jago actually have an appointment arranged, at a solicitor's or something? I mean, it was all planned?"

Mary nodded, squeezing her eyes in a fruitless attempt to prevent tears spilling over.

"He was going into town to see Tomlins. He'd booked a day off work and everything. He said because they'd been separated for so long, the divorce would only take a couple of months and then we could get married." Mary finally gave in to emotion and started to weep again, limp and helpless as the tears poured out.

Jayne knew she shouldn't have pressed the point, but this was the final piece of the puzzle—well, almost.

She had all the corners and most of the picture now. A few puzzle pieces were still waiting to be fitted in, but she knew. She knew *why* it had happened even if the how and some of the who was still a mystery.

"Oh, Mary, you poor thing." The whole table leaned closer, patting and consoled the crying woman again.

Jayne comforted Mary for a while longer, then made an excuse. "I just need to take Toby out for a few minutes. I'll be back shortly," she said, easing herself out from behind the table and taking Toby outside.

The evening had drawn in, the darkness gathering at the edge of the sky. A stiff breeze came off the sea, swirling a few pieces of litter around in the street.

Tourists still queued at the fish and chip shop, and the tables outside the other pub were full. But there was a chill in the air.

Jayne walked down to the green, in case Toby actually wanted to use the 'facilities' and took out her phone.

She called the Inspector. Was he always on duty? Would he answer, even if he wasn't?

"Jayne," he said, before she'd even announced herself.

She always forgot that mobile phones displayed the caller's name. "It's Jayne Jewell," she said anyway, the words already tripping out of her mouth.

"Yes, yes it is," he agreed with that air of faint amusement he often had.

"I've heard something. I think I know what happened. Well, maybe not exactly, but some of it. Most of it."

"You'll be putting me out of a job soon, with all this detecting you're doing," he said mildly.

"No. No. Not detecting. Just overhearing this and that and putting it together." For a second, she doubted herself.

Saying it out loud made it seem preposterous. And yet, it was obvious too. And there was surely nothing more preposterous to begin with than actually killing someone to get what you wanted.

Derek had been right after all. Follow the money. And

yet it wasn't just money, was it? It was passion and pain and rejection too.

"So… Are you going to actually tell me?" The inspector asked.

She'd been standing there with the phone pressed to her ear and her thoughts racing, but nothing actually coming out of her mouth.

She laughed. "Sorry. Look, I may have got this all wrong, but just hear me out."

"I will. And I doubt you've got anything wrong, Jayne with y. Now, tell me what you think you know, and we'll take it from there."

CHAPTER 34

Jayne settled herself back in the pub.

Mary had got over her tears for the time being and was talking knitting again.

Jayne got into a long, involved discussion about how to deal with the double cable knit that formed the basis of the pattern for the distinctive Marazion gansey.

Time passed happily enough and Jayne almost forgot what she'd done earlier. But the wheels she'd set turning were still moving.

Suddenly Katie sat up. "What's that? What's going on?"

Mary looked up. "Police!" she exclaimed.

Jayne could see them now. Two uniformed officers were moving calmly through the bar. Where were they going?

For a second Jayne had a sinking feeling. They weren't coming for her, were they? Some awful mistake where all her 'help' to the Inspector was actually interpreted as involvement, and knowing too much and guilt...

She breathed a sigh of relief as they glanced at the table of women and passed on.

It seemed as if every single person in the bar was tense holding their breath, silent, watching what would happen.

They made their way to the bar through the almost silent pub, approaching one particular person.

A Police Officer asked her name and then said, "I'm arresting you on suspicion of conspiracy to murder James

Jenkins, also known as Jimmy Jenkins, also going by the name of Jago Jenkins. You do not have to say anything. But it may harm your defence if you do not mention when questioned something which you later rely on in court."

Kensa looked around wildly, as if she was looking for help or a way out or even some indication that this was a cruel prank.

But next to her, Daniel David Penhaligon was getting the same treatment.

Jayne looked on, startled. *He* was involved? The charming, smooth talking estate agent?

Jayne noticed that everyone else had stepped back, edging away, creating a space between themselves and the two accused.

Was that just self-protection, an unwillingness to be involved—or did it go deeper?

No one was shouting to the police to stop, no one was throwing themselves in front of them and crying out that Kensa or even the suave Daniel David Penhaligon was innocent.

The crowd simply moved back, shuffling away, as if they didn't want to be associated with Kensa or Daniel any more. Was it a tacit acknowledgement of the real possibility of their guilt?

As the police officers walked Kensa and Daniel out of the bar, Kensa glared over at their table. Jayne felt a stab of guilt, but then Mary burst into tears again and Jayne felt vindicated.

Yes, she may have caused Kensa harm, but that was nothing to the grief poor Mary was feeling.

And if Kensa was innocent, then it would all come out soon enough and she would be back in the pub, glaring at Mary and shooting the occasional eye-dagger to Jayne too.

"Why have they arrested that lovely Penhaligon man?" Katie asked, aghast.

Jayne noted that she didn't question Kensa's arrest.

"They've been together a lot. Him and Kensa. And he's been sniffing around all the houses that my Jago—well, I suppose he was my Jimmy—owned," Mary said.

"Does that include the apartments where I'm staying? In Church House overlooking the sea? Did they belong to your Jimmy too?" Jayne asked, remembering the first time she'd met the estate agent.

Mary nodded. "We had plans for that too—to make it nicer, you know and rent them out to local people. No offence," she added.

"None taken," Jayne smiled. Yes, Penhaligon had definitely had his own, very different, plans for that apartment block.

"But surely he's not involved in poor Jimmy's death?" Katie asked, still in shock.

"Do you think Kensa *is* involved?" Anna asked, saying the words they were all thinking.

Conversations re-started all around the bar, people huddling in small groups, no doubt discussing the arrest in small groups.

Gradually the noise level in the bar rose back to normal, but the mood stayed odd, hushed, expectant and certainly not as boisterous as usual.

The women had all put down their knitting—stitches and patterns quite eclipsed by the arrests. Jayne kept quiet during the rest of the conversation, just agreeing here and there and asking the occasional question.

It didn't seem right to start talking about how she thought Kensa had poisoned her—especially when she'd initially blamed Mary and her pasties. And she didn't want her part in events to be too much the focus—especially if Kensa and Daniel David Penhaligon were released without charge and she'd been barking up the wrong tree.

But she had a deep sense of satisfaction. It was right that they should be questioned, at the very least. If Kensa had done what Jayne thought she had done, then she deserved the full force of the law. And if that nice man had helped, then he deserved it too.

It seemed like Kensa had been fine until she heard about her not quite-ex-husband's intention to file for divorce.

Until then, she'd been living rent free, and still had some kind of hold over her ex. But if he divorced her and re-married, she might lose her home. Would Mary have tolerated her new husband housing his ex-wife?

On the other hand, if he died while they were still married, she would inherit a whole lot of very valuable property and be a rich woman. And she wouldn't have to suffer the indignity of being thrown out of her home and see her ex marry someone else.

Despite her waif-like looks, Mary would no doubt have wanted Kensa out of the cottage and out of her new husband's life.

"What do you think, Jayne?"

Jayne was being poked in the shoulder by the blunt end of Anna's knitting needles. "About what?"

"Honestly, just because you don't live around here, it doesn't mean you can't take an interest. I mean, you're virtually one of us now." Anna was scolding her in a light hearted way.

Jayne smiled. She'd done more than take an interest, but it was best they didn't know.

"What do you think? Did Kensa do it? Is she going to prison?"

Jayne picked up her knitting again. "I don't know. I really don't. But I do know that love—and money," she added, in homage to Derek, "Can make us all do some very strange things."

CHAPTER 35

"Oh my God, Mother. You're wallowing. Stop going to funerals!" Tabitha exclaimed down the phone.

Why did she go from Mum to Mother when Tabitha was cross? She seemed to be increasingly 'Mother' at the moment.

"No, I'm not wallowing, dear. I don't wallow." Jayne had an image of a hippopotamus splashing around in the mud. Wallowing implied you were enjoying it. And she certainly didn't enjoy death or grief.

True, she'd been incapacitated by grief when Derek had finally passed, but that was exhaustion too. Despite the help of the nurses, those last few weeks had been draining, physically, mentally, emotionally.

Afterwards, she could barely get out of bed. She was horribly lonely. She was tired to the bone. There seemed to be no purpose or point left to her life. Caring for Derek had been all-encompassing, and now he was gone.

But there was Toby of course. He still needed his walks. So twice a day she would force herself to get up from her bed or the sofa or wherever she was lying in a sad, untidy heap, and get out of the house. And it did make her feel better. No, she hadn't wallowed then. Definitely not. And she wasn't wallowing now.

"There has only been one funeral really, it's just that it had to happen twice," she explained to Tabitha.

This second, proper funeral had been a much quieter affair and only a handful of the townsfolk attended.

Mary was there, of course, taking her rightful place as

chief mourner, inconsolable all over again.

Neither Katie or Anna had attended, both having decided that they couldn't close their shops again, not at the height of the tourist season when they needed to make money to last them through the long, quiet winter.

Most notable by her absence was Kensa. She had been the prime mourner at the last funeral, sitting in the front row of the church, dressed in black, her red hair cascading dramatically down her back. But not this time.

Jayne sat in the back of the church, with half an eye on the door. Perhaps like everyone else, she was wondering if someone would make a dramatic entrance—another long lost relative or wife or even Kensa, declaring her innocence.

But no. It had been quiet and subdued, as if the first funeral had soaked up most of the emotion and drama, and this was just the tying up of loose ends.

All the same, as Jayne followed the small group of mourners up through the town to the graveyard on the hill side, she got a shiver of sorrow. Was she wallowing? Reliving Derek's funeral? But if she was, it was helping. Each time, it was less painful, less raw.

She knew her own grief would never go away, but it might become more buried, less on the surface, and easier to live with.

She stood on the hillside looking down to the vast sweep of the sea beyond. It was a lovely, deeply dramatic location for a cemetery.

The view was wasted on the dead. But perhaps graveyards were for the living, and this windswept spot with its expansive sea view was the perfect place to grieve loudly and extravagantly, and to stare out to sea and know that nature didn't care at all, not one jot.

Her brain started ticking away again. This would be a lovely location for her book. Her heroine could stand here, the wind tugging on her hair, the grand sweep of the coast laid out behind her, and… But Jayne didn't really want death in her book. It was supposed to be a romance. Drama, yes, passion of course, but nothing as real as grief.

Perhaps her heroine could come to look at her ancestors' graves, and to confess her love for the burly hero. But he would be here too and overhear her.

Her heroine would talk out loud of course. "I don't do that anymore," she murmured to Toby. "Or at least, I try not to."

He cocked his head at her, looking up as if to say, 'You're doing it right now, you know.'

Mr Grumpy was there, with his ex-not-ex wife by his side. He'd given Jayne a sly wink when Caroline wasn't looking.

Jayne had smiled back, just being friendly, but Caroline had caught her eye and glared at her—as if Jayne had been caught making eyes at Mr. Grumpy.

Jayne looked away, secretly rather pleased that anyone would cast her in the role of scarlet woman—even if she was paired up with a man she didn't find attractive at all. But Mr. Grumpy definitely looked better now he was smiling. His nickname didn't seem appropriate anymore.

Of course, he shouldn't look quite so chipper as it was a funeral, but she knew he had his reasons.

Jayne wondered what had brought Caroline back to him— whether it was the shock of seeing her erstwhile husband with a 'fancy piece from London' or the sudden lack of any other options now Jago the first had passed away?

Maybe a combination of the two had been enough to push Caroline back into Mr. Grumpy's welcoming arms.

'Well,' Jayne thought, 'I've done some good anyway.'

The Inspector had been there, but he hadn't spoken to anyone. In fact, Jayne hadn't even noticed his presence until right at the end. She'd seen him standing at the entrance to the cemetery, watching from a distance, not saying anything to anyone.

"Yes, it was only a small, quiet affair," she reiterated to Tabitha. "Because the first one went rather awry."

"Dead people turning up at their own funerals. It's not right. I don't know what sort of place that is, but perhaps you should have gone to Rome after all. Or stayed at home," Tabitha grumbled.

Jayne smiled. Yes, abroad didn't seem quite so daunting now. But she was glad Tabitha had bullied her into coming here. It had been the most excitement she'd had in a very long time. "It's a lovely little place. It really is. But there have just been a few goings on. Nothing to worry about, darling."

"Hmm. Cavorting with murderers and dead bodies. I've read the news reports, Mother. I saw your picture. They printed your name! It's all over the internet. You'll never live it down you know."

Jayne smiled ruefully. She had indeed, for the first time in her life, been in a news article. Even though it was two weeks ago now Tabitha still referred to it as if Jayne had made the headlines of the Six O'clock News rather than one small picture and a single brief mention of her name as the person who'd found the body. It was hardly notoriety.

"Well, I haven't cavorted, darling. Not in the slightest. And I don't think anyone in Hertfordshire reads the local newspapers from down here. I doubt it's all over the internet. It was just one little photo and a tiny mention. I honestly don't think anyone back home will even know, or care."

Back home. The phrase felt slightly odd now. After her three and half weeks here, this felt like home too. The cafes, the pubs, the delightful walks, the friendly—well, partially friendly —townsfolk. The Inspector.

"Thank Goodness you're coming back soon. I checked the house yesterday. The lawn looks terrible and the whole place needs a good clean, right through."

Jayne sighed. "Yes. Yes. I'm sure it does." The thought of going back to the big, empty house, and all the housework that awaited wasn't terribly appealing. But holidays couldn't last forever, could they, otherwise they wouldn't be holidays?

And she wasn't needed here anymore. She only had a few days left and all the excitement was over. She should be pleased. She could relax properly and get on with her novel. But she had to admit, she was rather disappointed.

After the funeral, DCI Pollard hadn't spoken to her. He'd mooched off, his hands deep in his pockets without a second glance at her.

She'd hoped for another coffee invitation, or at least some congratulations on the part she'd played in solving things. Surely she deserved that? But the Inspector had turned on his heel and left.

That's the end of that then, Jayne thought, rather sadly, seeing him go without even saying goodbye.

Unless there was a trial, she probably wouldn't see him again. And he had no more interest in what she had to say. She'd given him information, he'd received it and acted on it appropriately and that was that. It was purely transactional. And it was over now.

She could just go back to her ordinary life. Home.

She sighed. She felt quite gloomy.

Home seemed a dark, distant place, chock full of memories she needed to escape from. Not forget. She'd never forget.

But she liked having new interests, new concerns, and Derek was still with her, talking to her, advising her. But the awful details of his slow decline and death were tucked away in that house in Hertfordshire and she didn't really want to go back and re-immerse herself in them.

She walked slowly back to the apartment after the

funeral. There wasn't a wake in the pub. The arrests and the uncertainty about who Jimmy had really been and the presence of the real Jago Jenkins had somehow put an end to that.

A message made her phone vibrate.

Tabitha, she thought, wondering when I'll be back and which train I'll be getting. The thought lay heavy in her mind.

But it wasn't Tabitha.

It was DCI Pollard. 'Can you meet me at ten am tomorrow, at Penzance station.'

She stared at the message. Everything here was tied up and finished off. What on earth could he want? And at the Police Station in Penzance? That sounded formal.

Guilt and excitement vied within her. She wasn't suddenly some kind of suspect was she?

She shook the feeling away. Why did any contact with the police force make her feel guilty?

Derek often had the same effect on people. Once he told anyone he was a Tax Fraud Investigator, people would get a shifty look in their eye. They can't all be fraudsters, Jayne had protested, watching it in action at a neighbourhood gathering.

Derek had laughed. "You'd be surprised how many criminals there are. Just because they're filling in a few figures on a spreadsheet rather than breaking into someone's house, it doesn't make them any less criminal."

Jayne still didn't believe it, and yet she had that same frisson of guilt as she looked at the Inspector's message. Was there something she'd done, or not done?

"I'm happy to meet you. But why? Am I in trouble?"

He replied quickly. 'Not as far as I know. Bring Toby.'

'Is he allowed into the Police Station?' she sent back. Last time she'd been there, she had had to leave him locked in her apartment.

'Not the Police Station. The train station.'

'Yes. I'll be there,' she replied. Now this was intriguing.

CHAPTER 36

Jayne walked along the coast to Penzance, where the DCI was waiting in the car park of the train station. She got into a rather scruffy car, the Inspector at the wheel.

"Given the way news travels around small towns, I thought it might be better to have coffee somewhere a little further afield. Have you ever visited the north coast moors?"

Jayne shook her head. "I don't even know where they are."

"You're in for a treat. It's a beautiful drive out there. Just sit back and enjoy the scenery."

Jayne resisted the temptation to ask him why he wanted to see her and what this was all about. Instead, she did as she was instructed, delighted to be taken on a tour out.

Marazion was heavenly, but it was nice to see more of this lovely county.

Soon, the town of Penzance gave way to high moorland, dotted with rocky outcrops.

"Oh, this is lovely. Very Wuthering Heights," she said, picturing her heroine walking against the wind, her long hair streaming out behind her as she went to her secret rendezvous with her handsome love interest.

Toby sat at her feet in the car. "It's a good job you can't see this view, Toby. You would love to roam around here."

Toby kept his eyes fixed on her face, saying nothing. She stroked his soft ears, reassuring him. She'd read somewhere that Jack Russell dogs look at their owners more than any other breed, and it was certainly true with Toby.

"The cafe does allow dogs?" she checked.

"Dogs, birds, adders and ticks, too, if you're unlucky."

Jayne frowned at him. What peculiar cafe was this?

The Inspector pulled off the road into a gravel parking area. He reached behind him and picked up a couple of supermarket carrier bags.

"I thought you might enjoy an al fresco coffee," he said.

Getting out of the car, she looked around. The sea was below her, stretching out into the distance, and in front of her rose a low hill, speckled with pink heather and yellow gorse flowers, with a well-defined path up to the rocks at the top.

Toby wagged his tail enthusiastically. This was exactly the kind of cafe he approved of.

"This is perfect, she exclaimed.

"Just wait until you see the view from the top!" The Inspector locked his car and set off, his long legs easily covering the ground.

She had to hurry to keep up, but then gave up and just stopped every few minutes to turn around and enjoy the view as she went.

By the time she got to the top, the Inspector had laid out two tartan blankets, a flask of coffee and a Tupperware box that looked like it might contain cake. He was sprawled over one blanket and he pointed to the other one for her.

She sat down, glad of the rest.

"You need the blankets. There are ticks and all sorts out here. You'll have to check Toby when you get back."

She smiled. This was a delightful spot and yet the Inspector was ever on the alert for hidden dangers. Perhaps that's what a lifetime of police work did for you.

She herself had been rather more hesitant about accepting any kind of food or drink from people ever since the

Angel's Trumpets incident.

Jayne tried to put it from her mind as the DCI Pollard poured coffee for them both. He was one person she could actually trust, through and through.

She gazed around. The rocks behind them towered up, weathered and smooth, strange shaped outcrops against the blue sky. Below them lay a patchwork of fields, mainly overrun with gorse and heather and bramble, and then the sea. Cars passed along the road, looking small and shiny, like little toy cars in a game.

"This is really wonderful, thank you."

"Well. Given the circumstances, I thought it might be better for you not to be seen with me."

"Because I'm a witness," Jayne said. "If there's a trial, will I have to give evidence?"

"Yes. Definitely. But that's not the reason. There's something else. I had a thought." He drifted off into silence. Then he sat up. "Let's have something to eat first."

"But…" Jayne said and then stopped.

Trying to curb her impatience about why the Inspector had wanted to meet her, and why he had decided they shouldn't be seen together, she knew he would tell her when he was ready. In the meantime, she would just relax and enjoy this beautiful place.

He rustled in the bag and pulled out a bottle of water and a plastic bowl for Toby.

Jayne smiled approvingly.

Opening the Tupperware box, he lifted out a round bun, sliced and ready buttered, putting it on a plastic plate and handing it to her.

"Tea cakes? Or a very belated hot cross bun, without the cross?" she asked.

"No. It's a saffron bun. They're a local speciality."

Jayne examined it again, hoping it wouldn't be as memorable as her first pasty. But when she took a bite, it was pillowy soft, somewhere between a cake and a bread, and with a golden colour, studded with raisins and dried fruit. The flavour was sweet, slightly grassy and earthy but with overtones of honey.

"It's actually very nice," she said in surprise. "Who'd have thought it?"

"I know. It doesn't look much. The saffron gives it an orange tinge. I think I did okay for my first attempt," he said, with a hint of pride.

"*You* baked this? Well, there's a hidden talent!"

He looked away suddenly as if he was somewhat embarrassed. "Well, it's my hobby. By default, really. I work odd hours, as you can imagine, and there aren't many hobbies you can do at various hours of the night. Any type of club or society meets at regular times and days which is no good for me. Woodworking and so on is rather noisy for doing at three or four am when I get home. You can't do gardening in the dark. So I settled on baking. It's good to have something to take my mind off the events of the day. And of course, I get lots of cakes. Bread too."

It was quite the longest speech she'd ever heard him make.

The idea of the Inspector arriving home at two in the morning and starting to bake made her wonder what kind of home life he had, so she couldn't help digging, just a little. "Well, that is an excellent idea. And it must save your wife from cooking too."

"I don't see why it would," he said, wryly. "She's been in the South of France for the last ten years with her new husband. I don't think my baking has much impact on her life, one way or the other."

"Ah. I see." Jayne ate more of her saffron bun. He was

divorced then. For some reason, the thought, 'Don't tell Tabitha,' popped into her head.

Toby was running loose, wandering here and there, following unseen scents and trails. She watched him for a while, enjoying himself completely. And she was having coffee and a bun on a hillside overlooking the sea. Simple, but very enjoyable.

This was a perfect backdrop for a romance. Her hero, the bronzed miner. She'd decided to go with that. Yes, he might spend a long time underground, but on the weekends, he would catch the sun and swim in the sea.

Her heroine would cavort over the moors with him, running hand in hand, climbing up to the top of the rocks. It wasn't Kensa. She'd taken on the role of vengeful ex-lover.

Mary was definitely the model for her heroine now. Fragile yet surprisingly strong and determined, willing to defy her family to have the man she loved.

Yes, that was perfect.

CHAPTER 37

"Jayne?"

She turned to the Inspector. He was saying something. "Sorry. I was miles away. I was watching Toby having such a lovely time," she said. It wasn't the time to talk about romance now, especially to the DCI.

"As I was saying, you're a useful woman, Jayne with a y. Very useful. You've got sharp eyes and ears and you don't miss anything."

Jayne snorted in a rather unladylike way. She couldn't let that pass. "I think I missed rather a lot. Like the fact that someone tried to poison me, for a start. I *knew* that tea tasted odd. I saw she'd been making stuff on the stove. I didn't suspect a thing. I even washed my own cup out—I scrubbed it clean. If I'd kept it, there would be evidence."

The Inspector laughed. "Yes. I've rarely known a victim clean up their own instrument of death so efficiently."

"That's what she did to Jimmy, isn't it? She poisoned him too." Jayne had to ask. She needed to know how the last few pieces fitted into the puzzle.

"Well poisoning would explain how they got an old sea dog like Jimmy into a boat at night and over the side."

"Do you really think that man, Daniel David Penhaligon, was involved? They could have been the two voices I heard on the beach. I thought they were both men, but it could easily have been Kensa and Penhaligon."

"I can't confirm that one way or the other. It's not my

place to influence your memories. But I agree that someone else had to be in on it. Perhaps you can speculate." He nodded, as if to encourage her to do just that.

"So, Kensa and Daniel David Penhaligon came up with the plan together. Kensa drugged Jimmy, thinking he was the rightful Jago Jenkins of course. She and Penhaligon took him out to sea and pushed him overboard, knowing he couldn't swim and he wasn't in his right mind either."

The Inspector nodded. "Yes, I Imagine he was probably unconscious at that point. We can only hope so, for his sake."

She tried not to think too hard about that moment—their desperation and the poor man's realisation. Yes, it was better if she imagined him completely comatose. He didn't know a thing about it and he didn't suffer at all.

"The poisoning explains the one tricky element of this case—the one thing that makes it a case and not a simple accidental drowning."

Jayne tipped her head to the side. "Does it?" She was still wondering about this. It was a puzzle piece that just didn't fit in yet.

"Yes. Your disappearing body—or to put it another way, why the body had to be moved once you found it that morning."

Jayne didn't quite see it yet. She took another bite of her saffron bun and waited for the Inspector to explain.

"If we'd found the body that first morning and had suspicions, we would probably have run some toxicology tests —basic blood samples and so on, just to look for regular recreational drugs or alcohol. Or we might have found physical evidence of a struggle."

"Oh, yes?" Jayne sat up a little straighter.

"And the blood tests could well have shown up traces of the poison—in much higher quantities than for any recreational use. And that might have set off some alarm bells. But finding the body days later—well, that's different. A few days in the sea, the natural processes of decay, the action of sea creatures, bumping against rocks and so on, it all tends to wash away any physical evidence. And of course, poison degrades in the system and would be much harder to detect. Even if we did find it, the levels at the time of death—and in fact, establishing the time of death itself—would be almost impossible to discern with any precision after that length of time. There are too many variables. The weather, the sea temperature, the action of the tides and so on. No. After a few days, they would have been safe."

Jayne pondered. It made sense. "And you think Kensa must have known that, so when I found the body, she knew it was too soon. The drugs would still be in his system. She needed him out at sea for longer. When she said she was calling the police, she actually called Penhaligon first and he dragged the body back into the sea. Maybe he was the 'Dave' who called her phone. Perhaps he was telling her he'd done it. And she told Officer Jefferies that I was a lunatic too, so he wouldn't believe anything I said."

"All supposition of course, But go on." He smiled encouragingly and took a drink of his coffee and dabbed his upper lip.

"Well… By the next time I found him, it was okay. He'd been in the sea for a long time. Like you said, traces and evidence had all gone. And Kensa thought she was safe. She would inherit everything, and everyone would be happy. Except Mary."

"And you. Because you knew what you'd seen that first day, and you wouldn't forget it. Kensa probably hoped you were a day tripper, or just here for the weekend. She must have been annoyed when you hung around for so long."

"Yes. Especially when I found him a second time." Jayne pondered for a moment. It all seemed to fit. Then she remembered something else. "What about the ticket—the ferry boat ticket I found on the beach?"

"Ah! The Clue," he said in a rather exaggerated fashion.

"Isn't it a clue?" she asked.

"As it happens, I think Jimmy and Kensa were skimming off the top with the tickets. She had some extra rolls and he'd sell those to the tourists, instead of the official ones and pocket the money. So she was about to lose that bit of income too."

"Do you need the ticket I found? I've still got it."

He shrugged. "It's not material to the case at the moment. That's just a side note. But an interesting one. I've spoken to certain officers about being more thorough around potential crime scenes, even if their key witness is 'verging on the hysterical' and 'not making sense' as Jefferies might say." The DCI laughed and she couldn't help but join in.

"It's not his fault really. I *was* in shock."

"And you hadn't had your coffee," the Inspector said, still smiling, pouring her another cup into the picnic mug.

CHAPTER 38

Jayne took another sip, her mind returning to Kensa and Jimmy and their ill-fated relationship. "Do you really think Kensa killed him, just because he was going to divorce her?"

"I'm not naming names at this stage," the DCI said. "But murders have been committed for a lot less. Of course, we still have no proof a murder has been committed."

"No, no, of course not. But *if* it was…"

"Well, under standard inheritance law, assuming that Jimmy hadn't made a will—and he doesn't strike me as a man who paid too much attention to the future or keeping his paperwork in order—then his current wife would be in line to inherit everything."

"No wonder Kensa panicked when she heard he was filing for divorce. If he died while they were still technically married, she would get both cottages. She'd keep her home. And those cottages are worth a small fortune these days, I suppose," Jayne mused.

"Not a small fortune. A large one. Jimmy owned Endon cottage, Primrose Cottage next door where Kensa lived, the jetty, and a very large swathe of the land behind it. And of course, there's Church House, where you're staying. There are what, ten apartments in there, half of them with a sea view? You're looking at millions."

Yes, there was money there, Jayne mused, and a lot of it, but passion and anger and self-protection too.

All Kensa needed was for the death of her not-quite-ex-husband to be ruled accidental, and then she'd be rich and free.

But if there was an investigation into the death, or any reason to assume it was suspicious, she'd be in trouble. She wouldn't get a penny if she was involved. The proceeds of crime and so on.

Derek had always been very clear about that. If crimes were committed, you didn't get to keep the money you'd made.

Of course, Derek was dealing with financial irregularities, tax avoidance, fraud and so on, but surely the principle stayed the same. And worse, of course, she could go to prison.

It was a gamble, and a big one, but she must have thought it was worth the risk.

Money. Love. Rejection. They were strong motives. Strong enough for Kensa. And she needed someone else to help her. Someone equally desperate, the ever-suave Daniel David Penhaligon.

"But why would a man like Penhaligon do it? Was he in love with Kensa?"

"I couldn't say. But I do know that his firm had been on the brink of collapse for a couple of years. A gambling habit and some bad investments can leave a very large hole in the company accounts."

Had Kensa got him involved in exchange for a share of the profits, or some lucrative property deals? While he wasn't the instigator, his involvement was almost worse. It was all for money. It was cold and calculating and purely about self-interest and rescuing his failing business.

Then Jayne heard Derek's voice again, 'Money is how people show their love, how they control others, how they take revenge.'

Perhaps Daniel David Penhaligon was more desperate than she'd realised. If his company collapsed, how would he face the world? He might have a wife and children depending on him and if he couldn't provide for them, he couldn't show his love for them.

Maybe Derek was right. Money was the currency of emotions. Penhaligon might seem cold and calculating with his involvement and his desire to get his hands on some valuable property at a knock-down price, but that could so easily stem from emotions of pride and shame and love too.

It might come down to following the money, but between Penhaligon's failing business and Kensa's marriage finally ending, there was a lot of love and passion and jealousy and rage there too. It couldn't be ignored.

"It's hard to think that Jimmy was wealthy. Why didn't he live like a millionaire? Why did he still work as a part-time boatman and live in that tiny cottage?"

"Don't forget that Jimmy had come by all of it illicitly too, if the new Jago Jenkins is to be believed. And his story does check out. He seems to be who he says he is—the elder brother, the real Jago. It seems that Jimmy really did assume the identity of his half-brother, come back from Australia and ingratiate himself with his ageing father. Jago's father."

"Surely his father would have known which son it was?" Jayne asked. She would know Tabitha anywhere. But if she hadn't seen her between being a baby and the adult she is now? Maybe it wasn't so easy.

The DCI seemed to agree. "If the ageing father hadn't seen them since they were young children or even babies, he wouldn't know the difference. When the father died, Jimmy, pretending to be Jago and with Jago's passport as proof of identity, inherited everything."

That made sense, Jayne thought. "But it still doesn't explain why Jimmy didn't live like a king," she said. "Although I suppose he was generous, allowing Kensa to live in one of his houses, and charging very cheaply for the apartments in the summer. I couldn't have afforded to stay in one otherwise."

"More than likely, Jimmy was happy to potter along,

renting them out, not selling anything. I imagine that he didn't want anyone looking too closely into his affairs. He knew he didn't really own any of it. Selling some of the land or houses could raise some awkward questions. He was sitting on a fortune, but he couldn't do much with it. And from the intelligence we've gathered, he seemed to be a man who enjoyed his life, just as it was."

Jayne laughed. "He enjoyed it a bit too much. Maybe that was the problem."

The Inspector nodded. "Having a good time can certainly make you a few enemies."

"But he was about to redeem himself. To get married and settle down, with Mary," Jayne said wistfully. If only they'd got their happy ending.

"Yes. I imagine that the pasty mafia put some pressure on him to do the right thing."

Jayne laughed again, then saw the Inspector was serious. "Really? The Pasty Mafia actually exists?"

"That's an exaggeration. It's just a local term. But no right-minded man would want to get on the wrong side of some of the powerful families around here, that's for sure. And if Mary's brothers said it had to be marriage, then it might explain why Jimmy was finally going to get divorced."

"Do you think they had something to do with it? Do you think they bumped him off, to stop him marrying Mary?" Jayne was excited by her new idea. Perhaps it wasn't Kensa and the suave property agent after all.

"That's supposition. But no, I don't. Jimmy was doing the right thing. He was certainly going to set the divorce in motion. Tomlins confirmed that was the reason for his appointment, but he never turned up for it."

Jayne found herself wondering about Jimmy and Mary. Would he have settled down and became a faithful, devoted husband? She liked to think so. In her story, he definitely would.

In the story she was going to write, Jimmy would get his happy ending. He hadn't been a nice man, not heroic at all, but he deserved a better end than the one he got, and certainly poor Mary deserved it.

She'd write it out. Mary, a thin slip of a girl, falling in love against her family's wishes, taken in by the local ne'er do well. But her love tamed him and settled him and he always wore the gansey she'd knitted for him.

'Perhaps she'll knit him several, I don't want him to begin to smell,' Jayne thought hastily, unable to stop reality intruding for too long. But he'll wear the ganseys she knits with pride and they'll be a happy couple, forever.

'If I ever finish writing it, and publish it, I'll send her a copy,' Jayne thought. 'They can have their happy ending, at least in my imagination.'

CHAPTER 39

She looked up to see the Inspector watching her. "It was definitely Kensa and Penhaligon?" she asked.

The Inspector shrugged. "Let's not name any more names. Remember, this is all mere speculation. But there will be a trial now. Let's just say, a certain party wanted to keep her cottage and would certainly have been glad to inherit a lot of other valuable property. And perhaps a certain other party was after an exceptionally good deal that could put his company back on the straight and narrow."

"And love, of course," Jayne said. "I mean, no one wants to be divorced and see their man marry someone else."

"He wasn't exactly her man. From what I've heard, he was the man of many women." DCI Pollard smiled wryly.

"Well, yes. But Kensa was the only one he'd ever married, and that had to count for something. The others were just dalliances, until Mary came along, of course."

The Inspector shrugged. "Speculation," he said, but he nodded as if he agreed with her.

"And Kensa didn't know he wasn't who he said he was— or that he didn't really own any of it all. If it had been ruled a simple case of accidental death and the story had never made the papers then the real Jago wouldn't have turned up and their plan would have worked. Kensa would have inherited it all. She would have been rich. And if she allowed Penhaligon in on the deals, so would he."

"But you got in the way, didn't you?" the DCI smiled at her, as if she had done it deliberately and he was impressed.

She wasn't going to remind him that her involvement at every stage was purely accidental. "So, when will the trial be?" she asked.

He shrugged. "We've presented the evidence to the Crown Prosecution Service. They'll decide if the case is strong enough to go to trial. Then they'll set a date. Until then, there's nothing more we can do. The two accused will stay in custody, pending trial. The charge is serious so it's unlikely they'll be granted bail. And then it's up to the courts to decide." The DCI set down his coffee cup, as if that was that. His involvement was over, and so was hers.

But if it was all done and dusted, why was she here? Why had the Inspector wanted to see her?

Had he just brought her here to chew over the case? Or to say goodbye? Or did he have other motives? She wasn't sure what answer she wanted from him.

She had to ask. "So, why am I here?"

"Like I said. You're a useful woman. You're an outsider. You've got sharp eyes and ears. You go about your business more or less unnoticed and unremarked and pick things up. It's useful. You hear things a police officer would never hear."

Jayne felt the ground settle beneath her. For a second, just for one second, she'd wondered if he had other reasons for bringing her here, more personal reasons. She wasn't sure if disappointment or relief was stronger.

Being useful was good—very good. She hadn't felt useful for a long time, not since Derek had passed. Even then she hadn't always felt like she was of any use. She couldn't stop the inevitable from happening. But now—now she was useful. Nothing else. Nothing more unsettling.

She smiled at the Inspector. 'Useful' was perfect. "So...I'm unnoticed, unremarkable and yet useful," she prompted him. Had he brought her all the way up here just to give her these slightly lukewarm compliments?

He laughed. "I didn't mean to be rude. I'm *not* being rude. They are all excellent qualities, to my mind, and ones I wish that more of my police officers had."

He handed her another saffron bun, saying, "We might as well finish these now," and continued talking. "Look, Jayne, the police can't do everything. All too often, there are cases we can't follow up. We know crimes have been committed, but the evidence just isn't strong enough. We don't always have the budget to follow up a weak lead or a vague suspicion. But I've been a police officer for a long time, and sometimes I just know. And it drives me mad when I can't do a damn thing about it."

She nodded sympathetically. Yes, she could see his frustration. It must be annoying. But what did it have to do with her?

"Having a pair of eyes and ears on the ground, picking up a few details here, a little insight there—it could be useful to me," he said.

"So, that's me, is it? The eyes and ears?" she asked.

"It could be. It will be unpaid. I can offer a contribution towards your expenses. There will be no responsibility, apart from checking in with me now and again, and not telling anyone that we're working together. You have to keep that quiet. The whole point is that if police are sniffing around, or anyone who looks in the slightest like a police officer, then people clam up. And everyone knows everyone else around here. Six degrees of separation is about two degrees in these small towns and villages. I couldn't put an officer into any one of them without it being common knowledge within hours. But someone like you —an outsider, a tourist, an author of course, well, you have a reason to be there, and no particular ties to anyone. It could work, you know, if you're interested."

Jayne could already hear Tabitha's outraged tones. 'An undercover officer! An informant! Mother! How could you!

That's dangerous. You're not qualified. You won't be able to do it. Have you got this right? He really wants *you* to do it?' In her head, Tabitha's outrage was replaced by incredulity at the thought of her mother ever doing anything so interesting. Yes, it would be an awkward conversation.

Jayne found herself smiling, almost looking forward to it.

"I don't know if you're free to do it. I was thinking you could start in a month or two. There's something brewing that I want you to keep an eye on. You'll have to come back down here, of course, and spend some time in the town and around and about. But like I say, I can contribute to your expenses, and writing your book is the perfect cover story."

Jayne smiled. The thought of coming back to Cornwall and getting involved in something, whatever it was, was exciting.

Having finished his second bun, the DCI picked a long stalk of grass and was peeling off the outer leaves. Reaching the centre, he put it in his mouth and chewed slowly on it.

Jayne smiled. She'd done the same as a child, until she'd seen a neighbour's dog relieving itself all over the patch of grass she'd selected the stalk from.

The Inspector stared off into the distance.

Toby ran back to her and nudged excitedly against her hand, wanting to be petted. "What do you think, Toby?" she asked.

He wagged his tail.

So that was a yes from Toby.

Derek had told her not to waste her life. He might even be proud of her. After all, he'd spent his life in investigations of one sort or another, following the money, finding the criminals. Now she could take on his mantle and carry on the tradition. She clasped the locket around her neck.

Yes. Derek would like that. He'd be proud of her.

"Well, yes. I think I might be interested, Inspector. Tell me more."

The End

CORNISH PASTY RECIPE

The Cornish pasty is a semi-circular flat pie, with a crimped edge and a filling of meat and vegetables. This is the traditional recipe but you can substitute other meats, fish or vegetables for the traditional beef steak or mince filling.

Legend has it that the pasty was the lunch food for the miners — they would use the crimped crust like a handle, holding it with their dirty hands, and discarding the crust at the end. Some say one end was filled with the usual savoury filling, and the other end had jam in it, to provide a two-in-one meal.

This recipe will make six average-sized pasties—not as big as Trelawney's pasties!

And there's no poison at all in this recipe!

Shortcrust pastry

500 grams of strong white bread flour or all-purpose flour

1 teaspoon salt

280 grams of hard fat, preferably butter, or a mix of butter and lard

Cold water to mix

1 beaten egg or some milk to glaze the pastry

The filling

400 grams of beef skirt steak or sirloin steak. Cut it into

small pieces about 1cm square. Low fat minced / ground beef can also be used.

450 grams (1 pound) of potato - preferably a waxy potato variety like Maris Peer, peeled and diced.

150 grams of yellow turnip (sometimes known as swede or rutabaga), peeled and diced.

150 grams of yellow / white onion, peeled and sliced

Salt and black pepper to season the filling

Making and baking

1.   Add the salt to the flour.

2.   Rub in the fat, until it is at the fine breadcrumb stage.

3.   Add enough cold water to make a dough.

4.   Knead the dough for a few minutes to activate the gluten.

5.   Cover the pastry in cling film or similar and leave to rest in the fridge for three hours. You can even leave it for a few days, or freeze it and use it when it's defrosted.

6.   Divide the pastry into six pieces.

7.   Roll out each piece into a circle about 18-20 cm (7 - 8 inches) across. You can use a side plate as a guide.

8.   When you put the filling onto the pastry, leave a good inch / 3 cm clear all around the edge.

9.   Put a thin layer of potato onto the pastry, then season with a pinch of salt and ground black pepper.

10.   Repeat with the swede, then the onion, then the meat, seasoning each layer to taste.

11.   Dampen the edges of the pastry with water.

12.   Fold the pasty over, so it makes a semi-

circle shape and the edges touch easily. You may need to flatten down the filling.

13.   Press the edges of the pastry firmly together before you crimp it.

14.   Starting at one end, press down on the edge with your forefinger, then twist it over to form a crimp. Work along the edge of the pasty all the way, crimping it as you go.

15.   Glaze the pastry. (This is a good time to freeze it, if you don't want to eat it yet.)

16.   Make a couple of steam holes in the top.

17.   Bake at about 165 Celsius (330 Fahrenheit) for about 45 minutes, until golden. It should be piping hot and the meat well-cooked.

SAFFRON BUNS RECIPE

Saffron is native to Greece, and commonly grown in India and the Middle East. So how did Saffron Buns become a traditional Cornish recipe? Some say the exotic spice was first brought to Cornwall by the Romans or even by the Phoenicians as far back as 400 BCE in exchange for the tin and silver mined in Cornwall. However it first arrived, saffron had become a common ingredient by the 1400s when there was frequent trade with the Spanish and North Africa. Saffron was grown in many places in Cornwall up until the 1900s and is starting to make a comeback with a few specialist growers.

This recipe will make 8 -10 buns. Best eaten on a hillside overlooking the sea.

Ingredients

300ml (½ pint) of whole milk (don't use skimmed or semi skimmed)

0.4g saffron strands. They should be dry and crumbly. If they are fresh and moist, dry them in the oven for 20 minutes on a low heat, so you can break them up more easily.

90g (3¼oz) clotted cream or heavy cream.

50g (2 oz) butter

550g (1lb 4oz) of strong white bread flour

1 tea spoon salt

100g (4oz) caster sugar - 50g for the dough mix and 50g for the glaze.

7g sachet of fast-acting dried yeast

70g (2½oz) of raisins or sultanas

30g (1oz) of chopped mixed peel

Making and Baking

1. Put the milk into a saucepan and heat it to almost boiling point. Then remove the pan from the heat and gently crumble the saffron threads into the milk.

2. Stir the cream and butter into the milk.

3. Set aside to infuse for about 20 minutes.

4. In a large bowl, combine the flour, salt, sugar and yeast.

5. Add the warm milk mixture and stir it in.

6. Knead the mixture for about 5 minutes, either by hand on a floured surface or in a mixer with a dough hook on a slow speed.

7. Add the raisins and mixed peel and knead it for a

further 5 minutes. The dough should feel elastic and bounce back when pressed lightly with a finger.

8. Place the dough in a bowl and cover it with cling film or similar.

9. Leave it to rise in a warm place for about 45–60 minutes. It should double in size.

10. Turn the dough out onto a floured surface and knead it again for a couple of minutes.

11. Divide it into 8 or 10 pieces and roll each piece into a ball.

12. Place them on a non-stick baking sheet, leaving a few centimetres space between each.

13. Cover with cling film or similar and place somewhere warm to rise again for about 30 minutes.

14. Preheat the oven to 200 Celsius (390 Fahrenheit).

15. Bake the saffron buns for about 20 minutes until risen and golden.

16. While the buns are baking, make the glaze. Dissolve the caster sugar in a pan with 3 tablespoons of water. Turn up the heat and let it boil for about a minute to create a glossy syrup.

17. Once the buns are baked, take them out of the oven and put them on a cooling rack. Brush the tops with the sugar syrup and leave to cool a little.

18. Serve them warm with butter or clotted cream. When cool, they can be halved and toasted and served with butter.

Thanks for reading. Look out for more Jayne Jewell Cornish Village Mysteries coming soon!

Printed in Great Britain
by Amazon

21642287R00129